MURDER ON THE SECOND FLOOR

MURDER ON THE SECOND FLOOR

By

FRANK VOSPER

♠

DAILY EXPRESS FICTION LIBRARY

Printed in Great Britain

FOREWORD

THE sudden discovery of an apparently cold-blooded murder in a London boarding-house forms the central situation of this dramatic murder mystery story.

Suspicion falls on various members of the household and every occupant is paralysed with fear. Who could possibly be the murderer? The very idea of such a thing happening in this respectable establishment is beyond their conception.

The tense and thrilling scenes written with strong dramatic force are, as the cookery books might put it, flavoured with splashes of comedy, wit and pungent satire.

On this same story Frank Vosper wrote a play which was one of the most popular successes of the season. Its drawing power was so great that notwithstanding the fact that the play had to be withdrawn from the theatre—the Lyric—owing to previous contracts, its run was resumed a few weeks later with increased success.

It would be the act of a spoilsport to give a detailed *résumé* of the plot. It is enough to say that not only is the interest aroused in the first pages of the book but is increased in crescendo as the story progresses. It is a baffling mystery with an unexpected *dénouement*.

Much of the action takes place on the landings and staircases of one of those well-known. "homes from home" that abound in the neighbourhood of Bloomsbury or as some prefer to call it—Gloomsbury.

The characters are cleverly drawn and are types that everyone will recognize.

There is the partly-obliging landlady, her husband who goes out to some mysterious daily occupation and often comes home with the suggestion that he might be in the wine and spirit trade, the old maid of limited means but unlimited connections, the industrious and hopeful author, the highly educated Indian student, and the tired and over-worked servant-maid.

Frank Vosper, who wrote both the book and the play of the same name, was the son of a well-known doctor. He was educated at Haileybury. On leaving school he joined the Army and served in the Great War. Immediately after being demobilized he joined Ben Greet's Shakespearean Company, touring with them for some time.

After a varied experience in the provinces he came to London and played a number of parts with pronounced success. His earliest writings were detective stories and his great hobby was the study of criminology. "A happy day" at the Old Bailey was to him a favourite form of recreation.

People Like Us, a play founded on the Edith Thompson-Bywaters case, banned by the Censor, was described as "One of the very finest plays of the season."

His recent tragic end, when he fell from the French liner *Normandie*, will always remain a terribly sad and grievous misfortune which cut short the career of a young and most successful author and actor.

MURDER ON THE SECOND FLOOR is his one and only full-length novel.

Murder on the Second Floor

PART I

MEET Sylvia Armitage. She is the heroine of this story. Sylvia is not reclining gracefully in a hammock, attired in a simple gown of flowered muslin, beneath a cherry-laden tree in a quaint, old-world garden. Neither is she sitting on a table, swinging her long, slim, graceful legs, with a cocktail in one hand and a cigarette in a long holder in the other, saying shocking things about biological urges to a horrified aunt. She is not even in a notorious night-club in New York, standing on a table, attired in less than half a bathing-dress, with a gentleman's silk hat at a rakish angle on her wicked little head, drinking her own health —in such liberal potations as must seriously impair it—surrounded by fifty intoxicated lovers in paper hats, carrying a dozen balloons apiece. No; at the risk of opening our story in a drab and disappointing manner, the truth must be told. Sylvia Armitage is washing-up. Yes, washing-up, in the scullery in the basement of a most ordinary boarding-house in a most ordinary street in Bloomsbury.

Sylvia always lent a hand with the washing up if she could find the time to do so, because Lucy, the maid, was not particularly good at washing-up. But Lucy was ever so willing. The most willing little person in the world, but not provided with very much in the nature of a will. However, if she hadn't a will, she had a "way." At least so Mr. Reynolds (number seven on the second floor) had said. Many a girl far more attractive and accomplished than Lucy has found a "way" more useful than a will. But if Mr. Reynolds liked Lucy's "way," Lucy was by no means sure that she liked Mr. Reynolds's "ways." From this we may deduce that a "way" is a pleasant attribute in a person, whilst the possession of "ways" is a doubtful one.

Lucy had an inferiority complex. That was not what she called it. In her phraseology it was described as "knowing her place," and her place, poor little soul, seemed such a dull, obscure sort of place as scarcely to be worth knowing at all. In fact, so unobtrusive was this "place" of Lucy's, that she herself seemed frequently to have some difficulty in finding it, for there were many occasions when she felt that awkward she didn't know where to put herself. When Mrs. Armitage deliberately "put her in her place," before the boarders, Lucy didn't know where to put herself. Again, when Mr. Reynolds told her that she was looking prettier than usual this morning, she didn't know where to put herself. So it would seem that even her "place," which it was Lucy's pride (if such a pathetically conscious humility can be so called) to know so well, had a habit, like most of her small possessions, of getting itself mislaid. But we have been asked to meet Sylvia Armitage, and here we are discussing Lucy Timson. If Lucy knew this she wouldn't know where to put herself, so let us leave her for the present comfortably in her place and return to Sylvia, whose acquaintance is decidedly worth cultivating.

*   *   *   *   *   *

Sylvia had finished her washing up. Not a very long job to-day, because "things" were unusually "quiet." "Things" in this connection meant boarders, and there were scarcely enough in residence at Mrs. Armitage's to be particularly noisy. There were only four in the house this week. And three in the family—seven large plates to wash up in all—no, only six, because Mr. Bromilow had missed his lunch again, the silly boy! Sylvia wished everyone were as fond of boiled mutton as Mr. Reynolds. His plate had scarcely needed washing up at all. He seemed to be the world's champion at eating such things as sauce and gravy with a knife and fork. Perhaps if Mr. Bromilow kept his strength up as assiduously as Mr. Reynolds he would be able to get his plays and books finished off and done with much sooner. Sylvia would ask mother to give them more fish. It would be good for Mr. Bromilow's brain.

"Please, Miss Sylvia," said Lucy, coming into the scullery, "I've helped serve the sweet. Can't I finish them plates?"

"They're finished," Sylvia answered, placing the last plate in the rack; "and you've disturbed my train of thought."

We, who have followed Sylvia's reverie, know that the train must already have met with a serious accident.

"I'm sorry, miss."

"That was a joke, Lucy."

"Yes, miss."

"What about the ash-trays from the smoke-room? I told you to bring them down."

"I know, Missylvia. I didn't forget, Missylvia. But when I went into the smoke-room just now, Mr. Reynolds and Mr. Jam Singh was there, and you know, Missylvia, how quick Mr. Reynolds eats bread-and-butter pudding, and Mr. Singh

never takes it, perhaps it's against his
religion, like so many other things. And there
was those two in the smoke-room talking all
quiet and secret like.   And as soon as I
come in they left off, and Mr. Reynolds says
wait till they'd gone down to join the others
in the sitting-room.   So I come away."

"Surely you could have fetched a few
ash-trays!"

"I was sort of scared. Mr. Singh was talking so quiet and mysterious.   And he don't
look so queer with that turbine on his head.
When Indian gentlemen talk mysterious—
in a sort of undercurrent, as you might say
—you never know what they might be up
to.   They might be starting another war
for all *we* know."

Sylvia laughed.

"My dear Lucy," she said, "I've seen
those two with their heads together before.
You see Mr. Singh has travelled a lot."

"Oh, but Missylvia, he couldn't never
have travelled as much as what Mr.
Reynolds has, him so much older than Mr.
Singh and been a traveller all his life."

"Yes; but as Mr. Bromilow said the
other day, Mr. Jam Singh has travelled in
four continents, and Mr. Reynolds has only
travelled in one line.   If you ask me, Lucy,
I think Mr. Reynolds is very curious about
the customs of other countries.   *You* know.

Er . . . marriage customs, and all that
sort of thing."

"P'raps it's marriage customs they talk
about so, Missylvia. Anyhow, it's *some-thing* wicked, I'm sure of that. The Indians,
now, Missylvia. They say, ooh! They say
they can throw a rope into nowhere like,
and make it stop there. That ain't right,
and it ain't natural. But, of course, you
been told all about that before, Miss, so all I
can say is did you ever hear of such a thing?"

"Why, that's only a conjuring trick,"
laughed Sylvia. "Funny you should men-tion it. We were talking about Indian
jugglers after dinner once, and I asked Mr.
Singh if he'd brought any special sort of
rope from India with him. He was terribly
offended and I had to apologize. I believe
he thought I said *dope*. And now you'd
better go and get the rest of the plates and
wash them up. And be very careful, Lucy,
you mustn't break any more things this
week, or I don't know what mother *won't*
say! Here, don't forget the tray!"

As Lucy went upstairs, Sylvia slipped out
of her overall. And very charming she
now looked in her dress of crêpe de Chine,
with its white bodice and green patterned
skirt, finished off with a dainty green sash.
She went into the kitchen, picked up a
novel, and sat down to read "The Crimson

Cross Gang," Leonard Swanage's latest thriller. But somehow, to-day, the activities of the Crimson Cross Gang failed to hold her attention. She wondered what Leonard Swanage would be like to meet, if he would be "nice to know." Was he young and "easy to look at," like Hugh Bromilow? It was rather exciting to have Hugh Bromilow in the house. Fancy having a real live author for a boarder, after the long, monotonous succession of commercial travellers, spinsters, and Indian students. She had lived in this house since she was five years old. Nearly seventeen years ago. Good gracious, how ancient that made her feel. Mother sold the "Bed and Breakfast" place at Euston, and became the proud proprietress of a "Full Board Residence" establishment in Bloomsbury a little while before the war. At the "Bed and Breakfast" place they had never spoken of "boarders"—the birds of passage who slept and breakfasted there had always been called "lets." Sylvia vaguely remembered nice "lets" and nasty "lets"; "lets" who gave trouble and "lets" who did not. And when Mrs. Armitage moved to Bloomsbury, and the long procession of commercial travellers, spinsters, and Indian students began, it was a long time before she could break herself of the

habit of referring to her patrons as "lets."
In those far-off days Sylvia had been
familiar with the song: "Let's all go down
the Strand." She had never then seen the
Strand, but had always pictured it as a
thoroughfare perpetually thronged with a
crowd of commercial travellers, spinsters
and Indian students.

Again Sylvia tried to read. She wondered
why Hugh Bromilow didn't write *nice*
books, like the "Crimson Cross Gang," and
make lots and lots of money. If she were
an authoress *she* would. But if Hugh—
she always thought of him as "Hugh" now
—became successful, he would cease to be
a boarder, and Bloomsbury would know
him no more. Perhaps that would be all
for the best, Sylvia thought. The sooner
the better, before she got too—oh, what
nonsense! As if she were a soppy, romantic
sort of girl. Nothing like that about
Sylvia Armitage. Certainly Hugh had
nice black hair, nice eyes, and a kind,
soothing sort of voice. That is to say,
when he wasn't "getting at" people. But
he was rather fond of "getting at" people.
Not that she couldn't hold her own. Trust
her for that! But Hugh—well, what a pity
he was so . . . well, so *superior!* He
didn't think anything at all of Leonard
Swanage's lovely books and plays. It was

naughty of him, just naughty, that's what it was, to shove himself upon a pedestal like that. And the poor boy had missed his lunch again. He wanted taking down a peg. Hadn't he any sisters, Sylvia wondered? And fancy going all the way to Strakers' in the rain last Thursday in your slippers to buy some more foolscap. He ought to marry. He ought to marry someone nice. Someone rather "highbrow" and artistic and terribly well educated who'd understand all his moods, all his queer likes and dislikes. No; that would only make him worse. He was such a dear, it would be a shame to spoil him. What he really needed was a sensible sort of wife who adored him but, nevertheless, saw through him, not too "posh," not too clever, not too unlike a certain Sylvia Armitage.

A piano-organ outside struck up a popular song. Sylvia liked popular songs, and she sang the refrain to the organ's jangling accompaniment:

"How do you feel
 When you marry your ideal?
  Ever so goosey, goosey, goosey, goosey!
How do you feel
 When the bells begin to peal?
  Ever so goosey, goosey, goosey, goosey!
 Walking up the aisle,
  In a kind of daze,
Do you get the wind up when the organ plays?"

The organ abruptly stopped playing. She listened. Someone was trying to send it away. What a shame! Such a nice, amusing song. Quite romantic, too, if you cared to take it that way. She heard the tinkle of a coin dropping on the pavement. How *does* one feel when one marries one's ideal? Does he exist? Now, *if* only Hugh——

An appalling crash on the landing above brought Sylvia down to earth in an instant. Lucy had dropped a trayful of plates again. Poor Lucy! Then Sylvia heard her mother's angry voice. A torrent of words—only a few were distinguishable.

"Clumsy girl! . . . my best dinner service . . . inexcusable . . .!"

Sylvia shrugged her shoulders.

"Oh dear, *what* a business!" she sighed. And Sylvia hastened up the stairs, anxious to restore peace. As she arrived on the landing, Lucy was standing and crying, with her knuckles thrust into her eyes, like a child.

Mrs. Armitage, for all her fifty-nine years, was still an imposing figure of a woman. She had been a very popular "principal boy" in pantomime in the days when a buxom, curved figure and a "dashing" style were the correct attributes of a pantomime hero. But most of the magnetism had faded from her personality as most of the peroxide had faded from her hair. But one of her members was as active as ever, and that was her voluble and sometimes venomous tongue, which had enabled her—in her salad days—to strike terror into the hearts of all stage managers, several comedians and even an occasional show-girl.

"Now don't stand there snivelling," she exclaimed, concluding her harangue. "Go into the dining-room and see if you can find last week's *Home Chat*. And if it's not there look in Miss Snell's room for it. I'm sure that's where all my nice ladies' books vanish to, and always before I've so much as glanced through them. Off you go now." And Lucy, still sobbing, disappeared into the dining-room.

"Mother, you shouldn't!" pleaded Sylvia.

"Well, isn't it enough to make you?" queried Mrs. Armitage, indicating what remained of several plates, cups and saucers on the floor.

"She's nervous," urged Sylvia. "She's so scared of touching the crockery. That's what makes her do it. She wants more encouragement."

"Encouragement? She gets more than's good for her from you, to begin with. Helping with the washing-up! What did I send

you to Woburn Hall School for, where you
mixed with the best set in Bloomsbury?
Did they teach you to wash-up *there?*"

"Nothing so useful," answered Sylvia,
with a smile. "You taught me that."

"Yes; when girls were so scarce"—Mrs.
Armitage was alluding to the servant problem, not to the problem of the superfluous
woman—"but not when you've got one,"
she referred this time not to her daughter,
but to Lucy.

"But, mother dear, we might do worse.
You know we might. Lucy's very willing;
she's never impertinent, she doesn't try to
'get off' with the boarders——"

"I'm not so sure," Mrs. Armitage interrupted. "D'you think I haven't any eyes
and ears? I *know* these quiet girls. They're
as wide as wide. Why, when I was touring
in Gertie Studholme's part in *Tropical
Blossoms* there was a meek and mild little
mouse of a girl in the chorus, and believe
me . . . well, it's not the sort of thing I
care to discuss with daughters——" Mrs.
Armitage often referred to Sylvia as if she
were twins—"but you can't get away from
it, Mr. Reynolds actually *notices* her. No
man would ever notice Lucy if she had not
gone out of her way to make him."

It looked as if Lucy was in danger of
meeting with another kind of notice.

"Mother, don't be absurd.   Mr. Reynolds would notice anything in skirts."

Mrs. Armitage crimsoned beneath her powder.

"Well!" she exclaimed, "that's a nice thing to say, Sylvia, I *must* say!   When you know perfectly well that when my figure was a household word as a 'boy,' when I was still a mere slip of a girl in all the number-one towns in the United Kingdom, though I didn't know it at the time, Mr. Reynolds was one of my most ardent and devoted admirers.   Anything in skirts, indeed!"

"Oh, mother darling!" protested Sylvia, "I didn't mean you!   You *weren't* in skirts, were you?"

"'To the pure all things are pure,' if it comes to that," replied Mrs. Armitage impressively, thus establishing the purity of her own erstwhile motives for exhibiting her physical charms, and of Mr. Reynolds's contemporaneous admiration of them.

"Then why shouldn't Mr. Reynolds 'notice' Lucy?" asked Sylvia, logically.

"Because Lucy isn't *there* to be noticed. I *was*.   It was my business, my profession, my work, my gift from the Almighty.   And it's not only Mr. Reynolds she's after; on the quiet, I don't mind telling you, Sylvia. Why, Mr. Bromilow——"

"Mr. Bromilow's nice to everyone,

mother. Why he even goes out of his way to be decent to Miss Snell."

"Mr. Bromilow has a motive, my dear," Mrs. Armitage asserted. "Always look for a motive. He's nice to everyone, so as they won't want to disturb him when he starts his scribbling in the sitting-room—which is definitely against the agreement—on Saturday afternoons. My word, I hope he's not there now, and me sending the girl in. *Is* he?"

"How should *I* know?" There was more than a hint of resentment in Sylvia's tone.

"Well, girls will be girls," was her mother's cryptic reply. "And I must say he's quite an attractive young man, and obviously doesn't drink his fees like most authors do. Though I doubt if he could write up a pantomime, even with last year's book as a foundation. But there's plenty of fish in the sea without anyone artistic, because they're nine out of ten from poverty corner, take it from me. So I hope it doesn't get serious, though I don't suppose the room would be empty long."

"Mummy darling, if I were serious about any of the boarders, I should have to get *you* out of the way, somehow."

"Who's kissed the Blarney Stone?" laughed Mrs. Armitage. She was beginning to thaw. "And, as you say, you might do worse. Susan Greenfield drank; Mrs. Smith wasn't married; and I'm sure the less said about Christina Bundy the better. And as for Mary Simmons and the policeman, well . . . *Listen!*"

Sylvia listened. She could hear Hugh Bromilow's voice. He was talking to Lucy in the dining-room. Mrs. Armitage smiled indulgently.

"I *thought* she was a long time finding that *Home Chat*," she said. "Ah, well! It's not to be wondered at. Sylvia, hadn't you better. . . ?"

"It's no concern of mine, mother."

"Well, your father must have made the coffee by now. Tell her to come and help me serve it."

Fearing that Lucy might get into further trouble, Sylvia obediently went into the dining-room. Mrs. Armitage, with difficulty—with very considerable difficulty—stooped to gather up the fragments of broken earthenware that decorated the landing.

*　　*　　*　　*　　*　　*

Hugh Bromilow sat in the sitting-room at 92 Malim Street, Bloomsbury. He was quite oblivious of the fact that it was Saturday afternoon, and that his fellow-boarders would shortly be invading his privacy. He had no idea that he had not lunched. He was only aware that he was trying to write a play—a play in the "grand manner," a literary masterpiece that might place his name on a level with that of Rostand, Maeterlinck and D'Annunzio. With a sigh, he threw down his pen, picked up the last sheet of smooth, white paper that had fallen a victim to the desecrating ink, and read aloud:

"This, then, Brother François, is the end. Failure, the world will say, if it says anything, and yet I am well content. Here is peace. Through the window of my cell too faintly comes the lark's song to steal the tranquillity from my"—he hesitated—"my —er—something soul. I speak—oh, damn the organ!"

For a street organ suddenly shattered the silence, and certainly stole the tranquillity from Hugh Bromilow's soul. He hurried to the open window, taking a coin from his pocket. He shouted in vain to the musician below.

A sort of duet ensued, Hugh shouting, whilst the organ steadily ground out the refrain:

"How do you feel
    When you marry your ideal?"

"Hi!" shouted Hugh.

"Ever so goosey——"

"Please, if you don't mind . . ." Hugh pleaded, feeling ever so embarrassed.

> "How do you feel
> When the bells begin to peal
> Ever so——"

"Would you mind . . . I mean to say, I'm trying to. . . ."

> "Walking up the aisle,
> In a kind of daze,
> Do you get the wind up when the organ plays?"

"*Hi!*" He positively yelled, in sheer desperation. The music stopped. The instrumentalist looked up resentfully at his interrupter.

Hugh felt rather mean. After all, if the organ-grinder was interrupting Hugh at his work, wasn't Hugh interrupting the organ-grinder at his? Still Hugh was in a position to compensate the fellow, and the fellow was quite unable to compensate him.

"I'm so sorry!" Hugh explained, apologetically. "But would you mind moving further up the street? A good deal further. I'm writing, and it's rather disturbing."

He threw a shilling into the street, and the instrumentalist moved off, vowing to return and interrupt this generous stranger again in the near future.

Hugh returned to the table, picked up his manuscript, and continued to read aloud:

"Through the window of my cell too faintly comes the lark's song to steal the tranquillity of my—er—something soul." The adjective he was groping for still eluded him. "I'll fix that afterwards," he murmured.

"I speak, oh, believe me, my brother, in all humility. But that tranquillity was not easily won. I treasure it, not in pride, but in deep thankfulness. It is hard, Brother François, to put away the world, to rise above a broken heart. . . ."

An appalling crash on the landing brought Hugh down to earth in an instant. Lucy had dropped a trayful of plates again. Poor Lucy! Then Hugh heard Mrs. Armitage's angry voice. A torrent of words, only a few were distinguishable.

"Clumsy girl! . . . my best dinner service . . . inexcusable!"

"Oh, my God!" exclaimed Hugh. Then, with a grim determination to ignore all future interruptions, he began once more to declaim more loudly and dramatically.

"Yet I have conquered—to Him be the glory—I have saved something from the wreckage."

On the other side of the door, Mrs.

Armitage had just noted that four plates, three coffee cups and one saucer remained intact amid the debris resulting from Lucy's mishap.

Hugh continued to declaim, with more or less appropriate gestures:

"I have saved something from the wreckage—myself! My freedom, and my living heart. These I gladly give now with a song upon my lips. Surely he will accept and be. . . ."

The door opened and Lucy entered the room sobbing noisily. Her knuckles were thrust into her eyes, and she was so absorbed in her distress that she was quite unconscious of Hugh's presence. For a while her sobs and snivelling continued unabated, greatly to Hugh's embarrassment. He was naturally a prey to nervousness, and had acquired a habit of disguising this defect under a convincing veneer of flippancy and unconcern. But on this occasion, when he at length found sufficient courage to address the weeping Lucy, his assumed lightness barely concealed his *malaise*.

"Oh, my dear girl, cheer up! It can't be as bad as all that!" he exclaimed.

Lucy started on hearing his voice and gasped with astonishment.

"Lor', Mr. Bromilow! I didn't know

that there was anyone in the room. I've gone and been and disturbed you."

"Never mind that. What's the matter?"

"I've broken some plates. Didn't you hear?"

"I did hear a slight noise." Hugh was most anxious to show a little of the sympathy he was feeling for the girl, but it was difficult. However, he valiantly persevered. "Still, it might have been worse, you know. It was only a few plates."

"I daresay," Lucy rejoined, almost forgetting her "place" in her distress; "but replacing them is going to make a pretty hole in my week's money."

This aspect of the case had not occurred to Hugh. He now realized that Lucy's annual income must be liberally perforated with pretty holes.

"But," he asked, "Mrs. Armitage won't make you replace them, will she?"

"Won't she just! You don't know the missus. She'd make anybody replace anything. Why, if someone went and smashed the Crystal Palace she'd stop it out of their week's money!"

"I had no idea she was so forceful," Hugh said. Lucy too, he observed, was showing signs of suppressed forcefulness. He had never hitherto suspected that there was such a strain in the girl's nature.

"Ah!" exclaimed Lucy; "she hasn't shown that side of her character to you yet, I don't expect, Mr. Bromilow. You know people have more than one side to their characters."

Hugh applied the remark, in his thought, to Lucy herself. He thought of the starved, spiritless wretches who had been transformed into merciless harpies during the French revolution. The worm that turns often becomes a venomous serpent. Would Lucy, he wondered—this meek little maid-of-all-work—if driven to desperation, be capable of exacting some dreadful and satisfying retribution from her oppressor?

"As a playwright, that piece of information should prove extremely valuable to me." He produced a pound note. "Perhaps you will be good enough to let me pay you for it."

"Oh no; really, Mr. Bromilow, I wouldn't!"

"Come, think of the end of the week."

"Oh, really, Mr. Bromilow, I shouldn't!"

"Come now, don't be silly."

"Oh, really, Mr. Bromilow, I couldn't!"

But the treasury note Hugh proffered was a new one, crisp and tempting. It looked worth far more than a pound. Lucy took it timidly, as if she feared it might bite her. "Well, since you're so kind," she stammered; "but I wouldn't take it from any of the other gentlemen in the house."

"Why not?"

"They'd think it was an excuse for them to get fresh with me, but you're not that sort."

"Thanks." Hugh was gratified to think that Lucy had absolved him from having another side to his character.

"But the others!" Lucy continued. "Well . . . !"

Hugh was not anxious to pursue the topic. Lucy was inclined to be neurotic, and he knew how neurotics loved unburdening their consciences if they could only find a listener. The girl might possibly be leading up to some embarrassing confession—maybe of entirely imaginary misbehaviour.

"It's not so much what they do as the way they look at you," Lucy persisted; "that Mr. Reynolds, for instance. . . ."

"He seems very harmless and uninteresting to me."

Lucy began to grow a trifle voluble. "Oh, I daresay, but these commercial travellers are as double-faced as you make them. If you ask me, I should say that Mr. Joe Reynolds was capable of anything."

"You astonish me."

"And that Mr. Jam Singh! How Mrs.

Armitage can stand an Indian slithering about the house, I don't know."

Hugh smiled. Anyone more inoffensive than Jam Singh he had never met, nor expected to meet. Jam Singh had even listened patiently when Mr. Reynolds, who loved talking about food as much as he loved absorbing it, had given him an extremely long discourse on the only way to prepare a genuine Indian curry.

"An extremely mild-mannered student," he began.

"How do you know he's a student?" Lucy interrupted. "It gives me the creeps."

The door opened, and Sylvia Armitage entered the room. Hugh was not only in love with Sylvia, he *liked* her. He had often been "in love" with girls he didn't really like. Apart from being young and extremely pretty, Sylvia, he knew, was capable, cheerful and chock-full of common-sense. She was as nearly free from vanity as you could possibly expect her to be, and for a wonder, did not regard herself as a potential film star. She seemed quite happy in her environment, and was content to help her mother to "run the house." She would probably, Hugh imagined, marry some solid, reliable sort of fellow in a bank. A fellow who shared her enthusiasm for Leonard Swanage. Lucky beggar, whoever he was.

Clever girl, Sylvia! Wonderful the way she could light a gas stove without nearly blowing the house up, or pull up a venetian blind without getting the confounded planks all cock-eyed and "skew-wiff."

"It's all right, Lucy," said Sylvia as she entered. "I've calmed mother down now."

"Thank you, Miss," Lucy answered deferentially, suddenly remembering her "place" again. "And thank you very much, Mr. Bromilow; I'm truly grateful." And Lucy faded out of the room. Hugh felt absurdly shy in Sylvia's presence. And yet he had numbered many brilliant and beautiful women among his friends. Sylvia, he thought, must be the girl who put the "Bloom" into Bloomsbury. She was so bright, eager, alive and unself-conscious. He found himself searching for a phrase that might summarise her charm for him. "No frills—no complexes—delightfully normal. Yes, that's it! Delightfully normal."

Sylvia mildly rebuked him. "You've been giving her money, I suppose, to pay for the breakage."

Hugh felt guilty. "Well . . ." he stammered. "Just . . . er. . . ."

"Extravagant creature, aren't you? Still it was rather sweet of you. You've missed your lunch again."

He glanced at the clock. "Oh yes . . . I suppose I have."

"You need properly looking after, that's what it is. Look at your hair." She smoothed his disordered hair, maternally, without any trace of coquetry.

"My hair goes like that when I'm being particularly clever," urged Hugh.

"What's the use of being clever, if you can't keep yourself tidy?" Then, looking over his shoulder at his manuscript, she asked: "Is that the same play you were writing yesterday?"

"Yes," he answered; "the same one."

"You know I think you take too long over them." He had anticipated some such remark. Sylvia believed in getting things done. "Of course, I don't know much about it," she continued, "but it seems to me that all the best plays nowadays are written in next to no time."

"Oh? I didn't know," said Hugh, whimsically.

"Look at *The Horror* for instance. They say that Leonard Swanage wrote that while he was shaving."

Hugh was on the point of asking her if it was a play about a man who cut his throat, but Sylvia wanted to be taken seriously, and her wish was father to his self-restraint. So he merely asked: "Is it a good play?"

"Rather, it's been running a year."

"Oh, well then, of course it must be good."

Sylvia did not realize that there was irony in the comment, and she continued:

"Leonard Swanage made fifty thousand pounds out of *The Grey Death*. Just fancy! Fifty thousand! That's what I call a real play-writer."

"You don't call me a real play-writer at all, I suppose?"

"Oh, I didn't mean that," she said, hastily. "Really I didn't! I think you write very nice plays. That one you gave me to read the other day was ever so sweet in lots of ways. But it was so awfully sad. I mean to say after all that poor fellow had gone through, not to get the girl in the end."

"Fellows don't always get the girl in the end in real life," he said. He knew that the fellow who defeated his rivals in the love-game usually got the girl in the beginning. Really, it was about time he put his cards on the table and let Sylvia know. A few weeks more and she would be regarding him as a chum, and then it would be too late. Girls hate to make lovers of their chums, and seldom make chums of their lovers. His attitude should have been more lover-like from the first. This confounded shyness!

"Fellows ought to get the girl in the end,"
she persisted. "In the theatre, at any rate."

"If you say so, it must be so."

"Now you're laughing at me."

"Ah, no!"

"Yes, you are. It's the only thing I
don't like about you. You're superior,
that's what's the matter with you. You're
all intellectual and high-brow, and you look
down on poor little ignorant mortals like
me."

Hugh was staggered at the suggestion.
She didn't know how he adored her, hadn't
the faintest suspicion. Hadn't she any
intuition? He, to look down on this
radiant girl! The idea was amazing!

"Me look down on you!"—in the vehem-
ence of his feeling, all his diffidence had
vanished. "My dearest girl, if you only
knew!"

"Knew what?"

The moment was over, embarrassment
got the upper hand of him again.

"I mean you're quite wrong. I don't
look down on you one little bit, far from it."

"You make me feel as if you did sometimes," she said, her natural candour assert-
ing itself. "If only you'd be a little more
human. You seem to treat other people's
ideas, things that other people have written,
with contempt."

"You mean that I despise success? You're wrong, but I want the right sort of success."

It was a point of view that did not appeal to Sylvia. She liked this young man very much and, woman-like, wished to "remould him nearer to her heart's desire."

"You only want the sort of success you approve of. Why can't you be content with ordinary success?"

For the life of him he couldn't say why. It was the way he was built, that was all he knew. But there had come a time in his life now when he only regarded success as a means to an end. He now wanted the sort of success, whatever it might be, that would satisfy Sylvia.

Hugh nerved himself for an effort. Here was an opportunity, and he meant to seize it.

"I daresay—" he began courageously— "I daresay I could be content with the cheapest sort of success if . . . if. . . ."

He moved a step towards yielding to an impulse to take her in his arms, but once more his diffidence defeated him.

"If circumstances were different," he finished lamely.

"Oh, 'if,' 'if.' What a word it is!" cried Sylvia impatiently. "If only you'd write a real play, like *The Scrambler*. Why don't you?"

"Would it really please you?"

Sylvia's tone was softer, as she replied. "It would make me feel, well . . . easier with you, and . . . and that would be quite perfect."

For the moment the thoughts of both were far away, in a rosy dream of a possible future.

"Yes," Hugh assented, absently. "That would be quite perfect."

Then these two people suddenly realized that they were betraying themselves. Sylvia recovered her self-possession.

"What I mean to say," she said, evasively; "It's always nice to feel on easier terms with anybody, isn't it?"

Hugh agreed. "With anybody. Certainly." His tone lacked enthusiasm.

"You see—" Sylvia reverted back to the original topic of their conversation—"what you ought to do is to write about people you really know."

"Such as?"

"Well, why not write a nice, thrilling play about the people in this house?"

"My dear child!" he remonstrated.

"There you are, superior again. But mother often says that she thinks some of the lodgers are as good as a play, and, after all, mother ought to know, with the reputation she made for herself in the old days."

"If an author's honest——" began Hugh.

"I don't understand you. How can an author be honest or dishonest? It sounds to me like a lot of rubbish, conceited rubbish!"

Hugh felt suddenly angry. There were times when Sylvia's normality was more irritating than delightful. But he couldn't be angry with Sylvia for more than a moment.

"I say, look here," he exclaimed; "we're beginning to quarrel."

"No, I'm not; it's you who're so obstinate."

"Well, let's drop the subject and go to the pictures. It's a wet afternoon; we'll go to that new film at the Tivoli. It's a tremendous thrill—five hundred aeroplanes dashing to earth in flames."

"No; I don't want to go to the pictures. You'll only sneer at them all the time."

"I won't, really! Not if I'm with you."

"Besides, it's wasting your time."

"But I've been working hard all the morning."

"Yes, at something that will never be any use. Who wants to go to a play all about young men fiddling about for four acts, and moaning about their souls and going into a convent——"

"You mean a monastery."

"Well, whatever it is, who wants to see a

lot of talky, talky misery? I admire a man who does something big and successful, so that everyone talks about him, and says: 'Look! There's Hugh Bromilow, isn't he splendid, he's got three successful plays running at once'!"

"Get thee behind me, Sylvia."

But Sylvia was facing him, and continued to face him, squarely. Her eyes looked into his defiantly. She felt herself to be the champion of honesty and common sense, fighting against all that was futile, pretentious, and . . . and unworthy of so charming a man as this Hugh Bromilow.

"I'll tell you why you refuse to do it!" she declared.

"Why then?"

"Because you jolly well couldn't do it if you tried—that's why. You make out that it's beneath you just because you couldn't do it!"

Hugh was thoroughly indignant. "Of course I could do it!" he protested. "If I wanted to—of course I could."

"Prove it then."

"No, but——"

"Just to convince me. Have a shot at it. For me."

"For you, Sylvia?"

"Yes, for me!"

"All right, I'll do it!"

And at that moment Mr. Reynolds suddenly entered the room, followed by Mrs. Armitage.

"It's the caper sauce, that's what really does it," Mr. Reynolds was saying. "And you get it better in this house than anywhere else in the kingdom. I've been on the road thirty years, and if I don't know what boiled mutton and caper sauce ought to be, who does?"

There is scarcely any necessity to describe a commercial traveller who has been on the road thirty years, and who knows what boiled mutton and caper sauce ought to be. There are thousands like him, slightly florid, middle-aged men, bluff, jocular, and voluble, entirely without individuality. Mr. Reynolds, like the rest of them, was generally held to be a good sort, a good mason, a good judge of a good dinner, and a good salesman of the goods he had to sell. In his attire he adhered to the fashions of thirty years ago. The fact that he still wore a gold watch-chain, and a tie-pin that looked like a large red throat pastille rimmed with gold, revealed his mentality. Though he boasted that he kept "abreast of the times" in business, he still thought double collars were "new fangled," and that a total abstainer from alcohol was either an unmanly imbecile, or a secret drinker. He was "always ready with a joke," but the jokes were all of the ready-made variety, based on such obsolete legends as that of the wife waiting for a husband—"detained at the office"—with a rolling-pin. He honestly believed that if a cook surreptitiously entertained a policeman in the kitchen she would regale him with rabbit pie—that particular dish and none other. The pleasantries he levelled at Hugh Bromilow always had reference to waste-paper baskets and the weight of the editor's boot.

"I hope that dreadful noise didn't disturb your writing, Mr. Bromilow," said Mrs. Armitage, in her blandest manner. "Really, Lucy gets clumsier every day. I got quite cross for a moment, and I do hate getting cross."

"How's the play going, Mr. Bromilow?" asked Mr. Reynolds.

"Oh—er—progressing pretty favourably."

"I don't know much about plays," Reynolds rambled on. "But I can tell you one thing, pantomime isn't anything like what it was. Pantomime has never been the same since your mother left it, Sylvia."

"You're pulling my leg, Mr. Reynolds!" protested Mrs. Armitage.

"Not at all. I mean it. But talking of legs, I can recollect seeing a pantomime in

Bristol about twenty years ago—*Sinbad the Sailor*, it was—and the principal boy's legs were. . . .

"You're making mother blush," laughed Sylvia. "Was she very good as Sinbad?"

"She was the last word, I can tell you. Knocked us all flat. Wish I'd had the courage to go round and wait for her at the stage door."

"Funny, isn't it, Mr. Bromilow," said Mrs. Armitage, "that Mr. Reynolds should come and stay here, and then you see he recognized me from those old photographs in the hall. Ah, well! It's a small world."

Another denizen of the small world that lived beneath Mrs. Armitage's roof then drifted into the room. It was Miss Snell, at present the only spinster in board residence. A harmless enough fragment of derelict humanity, poor Miss Snell suffered like Cyrano de Bergerac, from a nose. It was too large for her and it turned upwards at a ridiculous angle. Though certainly good-natured, Miss Snell was completely convinced of her ability to impress and interest her fellow mortals, but in spite of her habit of quietly thrusting herself upon them, she remained the most insignificant of human creatures. She meant to be intelligent and cheerful, but only succeeded in being dense and dithering. Nevertheless, she considered herself to be a woman of spirit, and always remembered with pride that in July, 1905, she had gone straight up to a policeman outside the House of Commons, thoroughly determined to smack his face. That she had merely asked him very timidly if he could direct her to the Tate Gallery had never, subsequently, seemed to detract from the heroism of this adventure, though she never quite succeeded in persuading herself, try as she might, that she had actually struck the policeman. In spite of being habitually snubbed almost from her birth, poor Miss Snell had remained so garrulous and innately self-satisfied that, with the passing of years, she had developed into a most appalling bore. So it would seem that a surfeit of snubbing, instead of having a salutary effect, had, like a surfeit of alcoholic stimulant, merely flown to Miss Snell's nose.

"You lost something, Miss Snell?" inquired Mr. Reynolds.

Miss Snell was wandering about the room as if she had lost herself. Hugh was watching her movements with the closest attention. Sylvia noticed this. She had also noticed that Hugh had been watching her mother and Mr. Reynolds very carefully. Perhaps he always looked at people in that odd, absorbed, interested way. Anyhow, she had never caught him at it before this afternoon.

"It's only my library book, Mr. Reynolds," replied Miss Snell in her mild, high-pitched, ultra-ladylike voice: "I wanted to go to Mudie's this afternoon and change it."

"May I help you?" asked Hugh. "What was the title?"

"Thank you so much, Mr. Bromilow. It was called er . . . dear me, I've forgotten for the moment." Miss Snell began to simper. "I'm like that, always forgetting things. Only the other day I went to one of these big super films, and when I came out I couldn't remember the title—no, nor anything about the film itself!"

"You were lucky," said Hugh.

"Now then, Mr. Superior!" admonished Sylvia.

"Oh, I remember now!" exclaimed Miss Snell. "It's called 'The American Tragedy.' A very good story indeed, I thought. A little sad in places, but——"

Here Mr. Armitage had joined the group in the dining-room. No one seemed to be aware of his presence until he spoke and then only faintly aware of it, as if his voice were the buzz of a casual bluebottle against the window-pane. Mr. Armitage succeeded in being more insignificant even than Miss

Snell, because he lacked her volubility and desire to be noticed.   Short of stature, and with a positive talent for self-effacement, people were always wondering what Mrs. Armitage had ever "seen in him."   Perhaps—who knows?—there were times when comparing the portly, large, self-assertive Joseph Reynolds, with her husband, she wished she never had "seen anything" in Mr. Armitage.   A medical student who had once boarded at the house had invented a legend that Mr. Armitage was, in reality, a casual border who had originally booked a room for one week only, but as he was unable to pay his week's rent, Mrs. Armitage had seized him in lieu of it.

Sylvia was carrying on a private conversation with Hugh, whilst the others were exchanging small talk.

"Well, got a plot for your wonderful 'thriller' yet?" she asked.

"I haven't started thinking about it.   It won't take me long once I do start."

"You seem to be studying everyone pretty hard this afternoon."

"People interest me."

"Colourless people like us interest a genius like you?"

"They seem colourless.   Perhaps if we saw them in their true colours——"

"What are you insinuating?"

"Nothing. I'm just wondering."

"Just *wandering*. What are *your* true colours, Mr. Bromilow?"

"Lord knows."

"How do we know you're an author at all? From the way you're watching people this afternoon, you might be really a detective looking for someone you want."

"There's no one I want here . . . not in that way."

Sylvia suddenly turned away from him and began to talk to Miss Snell about the weather.

"Oh, Edward!" Mrs. Armitage called to her husband, "one of the bathroom taps isn't working properly. I wish you'd have a look at it."

"Very well, my dear." Mr. Armitage wandered to the door, and then drifted back again to ask: "The hot tap or the cold, my dear?"

Miss Snell was peering through her pince-nez at Hugh's manuscript. "And is all this writing yours, Mr. Bromilow? How wonderful! I'm sure I could write, but I can never find the time. I think play-writing must be more difficult than anything."

"I once started to write a play," said Mr. Armitage, meekly. "A melodrama, with a fine part for my wife, but I didn't get very far with it. I forget why."

"Plays aren't what they used to be," sighed Mrs. Armitage. "Dear old George Sims and Arthur Shirley. And it takes a clever man to write a good pantomime book. Why Hickory Wood's works are living still. Have you ever written a pantomime book, Mr. Bromilow?"

"Not yet."

"You'd find it very difficult. You have to leave so much of it blank to be filled in at rehearsal. That's what makes it such hard work."

"You never appeared in a straight play, Mrs. Armitage?"

"No, Mr. Bromilow. Always musical shows, but mostly pantomime. That was where I met my husband. *Little Red Riding Hood* at Bradford. I was playing Will the Woodcutter. Edward was playing the Wolf."

"I wasn't very good, I'm afraid," interposed Mr. Armitage apologetically. It was quite true. Poor Mr. Armitage had looked far more like a starving cat than a wolf. "But my wife was magnificent," he continued; "the finest principal boy I ever set eyes on."

"That's just what I've been telling," said Mr. Reynolds.

"I'd no idea you'd been an actor, Mr. Armitage," said Hugh.

"Well, I never was an actor much, I was just on the stage."

"But you did act in a proper straight play once, didn't you, Dad?" said Sylvia encouragingly.

"Well, not for long. I once played a week in *Charley's Aunt* at Hull. But only for a week. They got someone else after that."

It was a confession that caused a certain amount of embarrassment during the pause that followed, Jam Singh, the young Indian student, came noiselessly into the room. He was wearing a white turban, white drill trousers and a dark blue jacket. He was not one to ape the complete Londoner, but adhered very scrupulously to all that his religion and caste demanded of him. He only had a slight accent, reminiscent of Welsh.

"Oh, pardon me, I intrude somewhat, I fear."

"Not at all, Mr. Singh. Come in," said Mrs. Armitage.

"Please let me not interrupt your conversation. Do not be minding me."

"Well, I'll go and have a look at that tap," murmured Mr. Armitage.

"You've looked out your train to Brighton, Edward?" asked his wife.

"Yes, the six o'clock from Euston."

"Euston?"

"Oh, how silly of me, I mean Victoria," and Mr. Armitage dutifully went to have a look at the bathroom tap.

"Edward's so absent-minded to-day. He's going to some wretched Masonic thingama-bob at Brighton, and he's thinking of that all the time," said Mrs. Armitage, apologeti-cally.

"How very annoying," piped Miss Snell, gazing out of the window. "It's raining, and it's set in for the afternoon."

"Looks like thunder," observed Rey-nolds.

"Oh, I hope not—oh, don't say that, Mr. Reynolds," pleaded Miss Snell, as if Mr. Reynolds were a deity who had it in his power to prevent or organize a thunder-storm at will. "Thunder terrifies me. It sounds like the voice of—er—Providence, you know. I'm afraid I really can't face this horrid wet to change my book at Mudie's."

"Mudie's? I myself am going there to the British Museum reading room for an hour or so. Perhaps you will allow me to execute the commission?"

"Well, it's most kind of you if it's not too much trouble."

"On the contrary, a pleasure, Miss Snell. What book shall I obtain for you in its stead?"

"The girl at the counter knows what I like, thank you so much."

"Not at all, not at all," murmured Singh, as he departed on his errand.

"Here, what about a game of bridge?" Reynolds suggested. "Seeing that it's a wet afternoon. What do you say, Mrs. A.?"

"I'm willing. Miss Snell?"

"I'm afraid I'm not up to your form, but . . ."

"Oh, never mind about that," Reynolds interrupted. "How about a fourth, Mr. Bromilow?"

"Mr. Bromilow doesn't play," said Sylvia quickly.

"Oh, pity! Miss Armitage?"

"Miss Armitage doesn't play," said Hugh.

Mrs. Armitage went to the door and opened it. "We shall have to get Edward to make up a fourth. He can do the tap later." And Mrs. Armitage went in search of her always obedient spouse.

"We'll play upstairs, it's cosier there," said Reynolds, with a knowing glance in the direction of Hugh and Sylvia. "What stakes shall we play?"

"Oh, very low for me, if you don't mind," Miss Snell pleaded.

"Tuppence a hundred, then?"

"I must go and get my bag," Miss Snell tripped away.

"My corns aren't half giving me gip," said Reynolds crossing to the door.

"It's the wet weather," said Mrs. Armitage, following him.

"I suppose it is.   But I've a nasty feeling it means I'm going to draw Miss Snell for a partner."

Hugh was alone with Sylvia.

"Look here, Sylvia," said Hugh suddenly. "I've got something to tell you. Something I *must* tell you."

"Yes?"

"I've been wanting to tell you for a long time . . . but . . . well, it's a secret. But it's a secret I'd like you to share, because . . . because you don't understand . . . I'm not altogether the sort of 'Johnny-Head-in-Air' fellow you seem to think me. That's only one side to my character."

"Don't wander from the point," said Sylvia calmly.   "What is it you want to tell me?"

"You'll be terribly thrilled . . . at least I hope you will."

"I'm thrilled already."

"Are you?   That's splendid. Sylvia . . . if you only knew how I've been longing to tell you. . . ."

PART TWO

PART TWO

IT was late in the afternoon. Outside the rain was descending in torrents; the sitting room at 92 Malim Street, was deserted. The door opened slowly and Jam Singh crept very stealthily into the room. There was ever such a slight change in his demeanour and expression; but had any of his fellow-boarders seen him they would have been conscious of a very marked difference in the impression he conveyed to them. He seemed somehow more resolute, even sinister. A vivid flash of lightning lit up the room, followed by a rumble of thunder.

Jam Singh crept cautiously across the room to the telephone on the sideboard. He picked the instrument up, paused a moment and then put it down again. He returned to the door, opened it and listened. No one in the house was stirring. He could not be overheard. No one else would want to telephone during a thunderstorm. He went swiftly back to the telephone, and took up the receiver.

"Primrose Hill 6420."

His tone was incisive. His accent had almost entirely vanished.

"Hello! Is that Primrose Hill 6420?

Good . . . who is that speaking? . . . ah!
. . . this is *number seven* speaking. *Number
seven*. Yes, could you please give me the
password?"

He waited. The password came correctly.

"Certainly I will," he said in reply to the
next question. And he repeated a sentence,
part of some secret code, in Hindustani.

"*Babt atcha sahib, sub chees teck hi.*"

It seemed the person with whom *number
seven* was in conversation was satisfied.

"Good," continued Jam Singh, in a tense
undertone; "we may speak freely now, but
quickly, please; I may be interrupted any
moment . . . I have received my final instructions, and I understand that the stuff
arrives to-night . . . excellent, and the
appliances? . . . How much of the stuff?
. . ."

The answer caused him to give a low
whistle of surprise.

"That is splendid . . . but you will take
care to send a better man than last time?
. . . Yes, he was no good, too nervy . . .
he must be prepared for anything, you
understand . . . what time? As soon after
twelve as you like. Yes, I will be watching
out for him . . . one thing more, if there
should be any difficulty with Reynolds?—
you remember our last conversation? Yes;
there might be difficulty with him . . . I

may act just as I think fit? Good! I understand.   Then I shall do whatever——" he
stopped and listened intently.   A footstep
on the stairs.   "There's someone coming.
Good-bye."

He hung up the receiver and moved
swiftly away to the window, and looked
out, as Mrs. Armitage entered the room.
She was preoccupied and absent in her demeanour, a look of anxiety was on her face,
which she never wore in the presence of
others.   The sight of Jam Singh caused her
to start.   Her features suddenly resumed
their normal expression, or rather lack of
expression.

Jam Singh turned slowly from the window.   He too, was once again his usual quiet,
unobtrusive, inoffensive self.   But when he
spoke, his accent was again noticeable.

"Ah, Mrs. Armitage, your English
climate!" he complained; "I fear I shall
never become used to it."

"Yes, indeed, it is awful, isn't it? . . .
and in June, too!"   She crossed to the fireplace and rang for Lucy.

"You remember what Anatole France
says about the English climate?" asked
Jam Singh.

"No, I can't say that I do.   What *did*
Anna tell Frances?"

He was too polite to correct her.   "The

observation was," he replied, "as follows: 'Whatever the weather may be in England, the English will tell you that it is most unusual for the time of the year.'"

"Fancy that," commented Mrs. Armitage, wondering why such a remark should be worth remembering.

Lucy came into the room. "Did you ring, mum?"

"Lucy, do you know where Mr. Reynolds is?"

"I think he's in his room."

"Will you ask him to come here, please. I wish to speak to him—privately." She emphasized the last word for the benefit of Jam Singh. The significance of the remark, however, seemed to be lost upon him.

"Very good, mum." Lucy went out.

Jam Singh was again gazing distractedly out of the window. Mrs. Armitage eyed him with suspicion.

"I thought I heard talking in here, Mr. Singh. I was surprised to find only one person when I came in."

"That is easily accounted for," replied Jam Singh with the utmost calm. "I was repeating to myself some Latin verses. I have memorized a great many in preparation for my next examination."

Jam Singh did not seem to contemplate going away. Mrs. Armitage found it difficult to conceal her impatience, after giving him such an unmistakable hint. She crossed to the fireplace, and sat down in an easy chair with her back towards the Indian. This was done with a certain amount of histrionic skill, and conveyed as plainly as any words to Jam Singh that his presence in the room was not desired.

Unobserved by Mrs. Armitage, Jam Singh whipped a small note-book and pencil from his pocket, hastily wrote a few lines, and hastily tore out the page and folded it up, just as Joseph Reynolds entered the room. Reynolds remained by the door. He, too, looked at Jam Singh with a certain amount of suspicion, not to say hostility. Then he said, quite formally and unconcernedly:

"You wished to speak to me, Mrs. Armitage?"

"If you please, Mr. Reynolds—er—*privately*."

This time it suited Mr. Jam Singh's convenience to take the hint. "Oh! but certainly, of course!" he said, quite deferentially, and moved away from the window.

Reynolds was still by the door. As the Indian passed him, he slipped the folded piece of paper from his note-book into Reynolds's hand. Reynolds slipped the paper into his waistcoat pocket. As soon as he was left alone with Mrs. Armitage, Reynolds assumed a slightly domineering, half-bantering manner.

"Well, Rosie, what's the matter now?" he asked brusquely.

Mrs. Armitage rose from her chair impulsively, and spoke quietly, but her voice was vibrant with suppressed terror.

"Joe, I'm nervous; you keep me so in the dark, it frightens the life out of me."

Reynolds seemed suddenly to have assumed an air of almost brutal arrogance. None of his daily associates would have suspected him of having so much of the bully in his composition. Checking a desire to use angry, perhaps threatening words to the woman, he resumed his bantering tone.

"Come now, don't be so unreasonable. Surely you know me well enough by now to know that I'm not going to run you into any danger."

But Mrs. Armitage was not so easily to be pacified.

"You say so, Joe; but it doesn't stop me getting worried silly. Sylvia's grown up now. I feel that I have no right to let her——"

She suddenly stopped speaking. Some indefinable, instinctive sense of danger compelled her to move swiftly and stealthily across the room. She arrived at the door without making a sound, then deliberately and suddenly threw it open. Lucy, taken completely unawares, almost fell into the room.

"I thought so!" Mrs. Armitage grasped Lucy roughly by the arm and gave her a vicious shake. "You wicked girl! What are you doing listening at keyholes?"

Lucy wrenched herself free from her mistress's grasp. There was something most unusual in the maid's look of defiance and contempt with which she confronted Mrs. Armitage. She seemed suddenly to have acquired a certain dignity.

"I didn't mean any harm," she said sullenly.

"I don't care what you meant. How much did you hear?"

Lucy looked at the woman scornfully.

"Go on, tell me."

"I didn't hear anything, you were speaking too low."

"You leave at the end of this week, anyhow, my girl," said Mrs. Armitage, wishing it were in her power to inflict more terrible penalties. "You're nothing more than a mean, common eavesdropper. You'll just get your week's wages, and not a penny more; and now get out of here and go to your kitchen and stay there."

Without a word of protest Lucy turned and went from the room.

Mrs. Armitage was almost hysterical. "There you are, Joe," she said. "That's what it is all the time, watching and prying everywhere. I feel as though I had no one to trust; it's breaking me up."

Reynolds put his arm reassuringly round her shoulder. "There, there, Rosie, it's all right. Lucy doesn't know anything about this house; she was just listening at the door, like thousands of other servants do."

"Well, she's going at the end of the week. That's flat."

As a matter of fact, Joseph Reynolds looked on it as a great stroke of luck for himself that Lucy had been caught eavesdropping. It suited his book very well indeed. Lucy's dismissal from the house would be a great relief to him.

"Oh, certainly she'd better go," he agreed. "I'll put in one of my own men, someone we can trust, then we shall know where we are."

"*I* shan't. You tell me nothing, Joe; that's what's driving me frantic."

"Now, listen to me, my dear," he coaxed her, "how long has our arrangement about this house been going on?"

"About ten years—yes, ten years next month."

"And our arrangement was perfectly clear, wasn't it? You were sick of the stage, you wanted to retire, but your husband showed no earthly prospect of supporting either you or himself if you did retire. I agreed, because of our early happy days together, and because I still cared for you to take a boarding-house for you. First there was the little place at Euston, and then when my schemes matured and things began to turn out according to plan, I took this place on. My only stipulation was that two or three rooms should always be kept free for me to use in whatever way I chose for my—er—my activities."

Mrs. Armitage was growing tearful. How much happier, how much more peaceful her life would have been if Joseph Reynolds had never waited for her that night at the stage door!

"I only accepted because I cared for you, Joe," she protested. "I still care, although I don't believe you do."

It was one of the plagues of Mr. Joseph Reynolds's life that women went on caring for him. It didn't matter if you could tell them point blank that you were sick of 'em and they could get out of it to hell. But when you had got to pretend you still loved a woman in her late 'fifties—well, that was the very devil.

He patted her on the arm with a show of affection. "Of course I still care for you, my dear, you know it perfectly well. Anyway, you accepted my arrangement, which has worked admirably. You take in your lodgers and make a nice bit of pocket money for yourself, providing at the same time a very excellent centre for my various business deals."

"Yes, I know, but——"

"From the very first I told you—didn't I?—that I never by any chance allowed a woman to come into my schemes, and that was why they always went so smoothly."

"Yes, Joe."

"I was speaking the truth. During all these years—and I've brought off a lot of good deals in that time—there's never been a hint of trouble, has there? No police or detectives have so much as ever appeared on the doorstep."

"That's true enough," admitted Mrs. Armitage.

"Very well, then, what reason have you to worry now?"

"It's only that——"

"It's only, my dear, silly Rosie, that your curiosity increases year by year; you must conquer it. I know it's a natural quality in a woman, but you must remember curiosity killed the cat. You ought to be thankful that I keep all heavy responsibility away from you."

"I am thankful, truly I am," she pleaded. "But, you see, I'm thinking of Sylvia. When I began all this Sylvia was a little girl, but she's grown up. I'm terrified of her finding things out."

Reynolds dismissed the suggestion. "Why should she? She's not particularly inquisitive. She's too busy enjoying herself and finding her feet and making conquests."

But this allusion had the reverse of a reassuring effect on Mrs. Armitage.

"Ah, you mean Mr. Bromilow. There's another thing that makes me anxious. He's not like the usual type of lodgers here. He's about the house all day with his writing, and he's much more observant than most. Only the other day he asked me if I was interested in crime."

"That's nothing. Most authors fancy themselves as criminologists. You've nothing to fear from him; he's far too interested in your daughter to worry about anything else. Where is he, by the way?"

"He's taken Sylvia to the pictures. He asked her if she'd care to see the new film at the Tivoli, and of course she said she would."

"There you are!"

"He's taking her out to dinner and then they're going to something else."

"They won't be out very late, I suppose?" Reynolds asked suddenly.

"Oh, no; he promised to bring her home shortly after eleven."

"Good!" Reynolds exclaimed. "They'll be well out of the way before twelve, if you don't let them stop up talking."

Why should Joe Reynolds want Sylvia and Bromilow out of the way before twelve? She knew that Joe was going to be busy that night with his "activities," whatever they were.

"Ah!" she exclaimed; "I knew there was something brewing."

"Now don't you start again," he warned her. "How about Miss Snell? She won't be up late?"

"Good heavens, no. She's always in her room by ten."

"And your husband's going to some Masonic affair at Brighton, isn't he?"

"Yes; I think he must have gone already," she answered, glancing at the clock. "His train leaves at six, and it's past five now."

"Well, that's fine!" Reynolds exclaimed. His luck was holding good, as it always had done. "We've got everyone accounted for. You go to bed early to-night, and sleep soundly and don't worry your head about anything. You trust your old friend

Joseph. There, d'you feel more reassured now, my dear?"

"Yes, Joe, I do!" She looked at him, and remembered him as he was all those long years ago, handsome in a coarse sort of way, so blunt, so amusing, so unabashed in his overtures. A man who knew what he wanted of a woman and who meant to have it, who put his cards on the table. How it had appealed to her after the kid-gloved finessing of most of her admirers, the puerile chivalry of others, and the maddeningly meek adoration of such men as Edward Armitage.

"Of course you can trust me. That's a good girl; give us a kiss."

He kissed her at first with casual affection, but she clung to him and a muffled sob forced itself from her lips. Then he, too, remembered, and they kissed again, as they had kissed many, many years ago.

They drew suddenly apart. Mr. Armitage was in the room. He wore a check cap, which made him look more of a nonentity than ever, and he carried a small cheap-looking attaché case. A poor thing, like its owner.

"Just off, my dear," he said. "I shall get a bus at Southampton Row."

His tone was quite casual. Evidently, Mrs. Armitage thought, he had noticed nothing.

"What on earth d'you want to take that silly little case for?" she asked, with assumed unconcern.

"Dunno, m'dear.   Couldn't find anything else. . . . Hullo, Mr. Reynolds, you've not gone out then?   Obviously you haven't—silly question."   He produced a packet of cigarettes.   "Have one, Mr. Reynolds? . . . Oh, no, of course, you never smoke anything but your pipe, do you?"

"I don't mind betting you've forgotten something, Edward," said his wife, who had quite recovered her composure.

Mr. Armitage lit a cigarette.   "Don't think so . . . pyjamas . . . tooth-brush, sponge-bag, brushes and comb, dressing-gown——"

"How about your bedroom slippers?"

"There now!" exclaimed Mr. Armitage guiltily.

"Ah, what did I tell you?" Mrs. Armitage picked up the attaché case.   "I'll get them for you and put them in.   Come along, Edward, I'll see you off safely.   See you at dinner, Mr. Reynolds; I shall go and lie down, I've got a bit of a headache."

And Mrs. Armitage left the dining-room meekly followed by her husband.

Reynolds walked up and down the room for about half a minute in deep thought. He wondered how much that girl had overheard. He'd send for her and get the truth out of her. He rang the bell, and whilst he was waiting for Lucy to answer it, he read the paper Jam Singh had given him, then made a few rapid pencilled calculations in his own pocket-book.

Lucy entered. Her demeanour was one of sullen dejection. She closed the door, but when she saw Reynolds she stood, holding on to the handle, staring at the man with a gaze in which horror, fear and hatred were mingled. She was like some miserable, hunted creature at bay. Reynolds met her gaze unflinchingly.

"What the hell were you doing listening outside?" he asked, with quiet force.

Lucy answered contemptuously: "You know quite well why I was listening."

"I do not. I shouldn't ask if I did. I've no time for useless questions."

Lucy answered him steadily: "I was listening to hear what you and Mrs. Armitage were saying about me."

"About *you!*" gasped Reynolds in genuine amazement. "My good girl, why on earth should we be talking about you?"

"You mean to say that she hasn't discovered?" asked Lucy, just as much surprised.

"Discovered?" he said impatiently. "What on earth are you talking about?"

After all, the little servant girl had more moral courage than he. It was no time for equivocation.

"I thought," she said boldly, "that Mrs. Armitage had found out about you and me."

"Oh, so *that's* what you thought! I see! And you were listening so as to find out. . . ."

"To find out what was going to happen. I was certain she'd discover how it was with me, and that she knew that you were the man."

"Well, you were wrong, see?" said Reynolds callously. "Mrs. Armitage knows nothing about you and me. Nothing whatsoever."

Lucy began to lose her self-control. Her voice trembled pitifully. "It doesn't make much difference what she knows now. I've got the sack, anyway. I'm done for. What are you going to do for me?"

"Why on earth should I do anything for you?" he asked brutally.

Lucy left the door and advanced towards him with blazing eyes. "You can stand there and ask that?" she cried. "Can't you imagine how I'm feeling just at present? I'm going to be turned out of the house at the end of the week with only a few shillings, no work, and no chance of it with the character she'll give me . . . I've no one to turn to, nowhere to go, and then this awful trouble. You've got to help me, for heaven's sake!" Her voice rose higher as she spoke. It was a pitiful appeal; but it was made to a man without pity.

"Stop that row!" he said fiercely. "Help you, indeed! You've had a damn sight more out of me than you've got out of the other men in this house, and you're not going to get any more."

"But you can't let me down—I'm desperate!" Lucy implored.

"Good God!" exclaimed Reynolds. "Do you think I'm going to be responsible for a promiscuous little slut of a housemaid like you?"

Lucy was beside herself with rage and shame.

"You low hound!" she cried. "How dare you speak to me like that!"

"It's the truth, and you know it. Your behaviour in this house, and out of it I daresay, doesn't warrant your fastening the responsibility for your troubles on to any-one."

Lucy had not overstated the case when she had said that she was desperate, and this man's cruelly callous attitude was sheer torture.

"It's you, I swear it is!" she persisted. "I'm not asking much—just a little support till it's all over."

"I don't care what you're asking, you're not going to get it. Women who play your game have got to take the consequences, and that's all there is to it."

Lucy turned on him furiously. "Then I shall have to find a way to make you help me. I shall tell everyone."

"And who'd believe you?" he retorted. "It would simply mean that you'd be turned out on the streets to-night instead of the end of the week. You poor little fool, trying to blackmail me; you don't know what you're up against!"

Her answer came as a bit of a shock to him. "No, I don't, and that's a fact!" she declared. "There's something strange about you and the whole of this house."

He suddenly seized the girl roughly by the wrist and peered into her eyes. "My God!" he cried, "I believe you were listening at that door for some other reason. Come on now, out with it—how much do you know?"

"I don't know anything—I don't!"

"If I thought you did I'd choke the life out of you here and now."

Lucy was terrified. "I swear I wasn't trying to find out anything but what I told you," she vowed. "I swear it!" She uttered a sharp cry of pain. "Let me go— you're hurting my wrist!"

He relaxed his cruel grip. "Let this be a warning to you, then," he threatened. "But if I catch you prying into anything that doesn't concern you, I won't answer for what may happen to you. Now clear out."

Lucy drifted to the door, then suddenly burst into a torrent of bitter sobs.

"Stop that damn row and get out of here," said Reynolds ferociously.

The girl choked back her sobs, and spoke with a sudden access of desperate courage.

"All right, Mr. Joseph Reynolds, I'll go. You think you've got away with it, with your cowardly bullying, don't you?"

"Get out!" he snarled.

Lucy was almost demented by rage and misery. Her anguish was painful to witness. "Blast you," she cried, "I tell you you haven't got away with it. I'll get back on you, I swear I will. I'm sick of you and your sort, and the way you treat women. You're right! There's been dozens of other men in this house before you, and I feel mad with shame at myself when I look back on them. Just a pack of low, greedy beasts, taking what they want and chucking you aside. You're the worst of the lot, an' you're going to pay for it. I've got nothing more to lose, whatever happens now. I'm desperate, and I'll stick at nothing; so look out for yourself, you dirty swine, you

haven't finished with me yet!" Lucy
slammed the door. Reynolds was alone.

"Lot of theatrical nonsense!" he muttered
contemptuously.

* * * * * *

Strange, was it not, that all this time
Sylvia was enjoying herself immensely.
In later years she was destined to remember
this dismal, wet afternoon as one of the
happiest in her life. Hugh had at last
"come out of his shell," and Sylvia found
that she could listen to every word he
uttered with profound interest. It was
the first time he had ever devoted an
entire afternoon to her amusement—that,
in itself, was sufficiently thrilling. But no
other man yet who had courted her society
had ever been able to amuse and entertain
her as Hugh did, in a manner so original,
so intriguing, so delightfully absorbing. His
keen imagination, she discovered, was re-
inforced by a hitherto unsuspected gift of
mimicry that made his description of people
and events vivid and convincing. She now
clearly saw that his flippancy, his aloof-
ness, his "superiority" were, so to speak, the
colours of which he composed a camou-
flage for his shyness. That afternoon he
became frank, enthusiastic, intimate,
human. And Hugh, for his part, who had
thought it so fine a thing to interest

thousands of people he would never meet, was finding it sweeter to interest this one girl whom he had learned to love better than he could ever love success—even the right sort of success!

*   *   *   *   *   *

If you stood on the landing of the first floor at No. 92 Malim Street, Bloomsbury, looking upwards towards the second floor, with your back towards the windows that looked out into the street, immediately to your right would be a flight of stairs leading to the landing of the second floor. A little further to the left, on the first floor, was the room occupied by Hugh Bromilow. The room immediately above Hugh's on the second floor was Miss Snell's. Facing you would be the landing of the second floor, with the door of Mr. Reynolds' bedroom in the centre. A little to the left of this door you would see a flight of stairs which led to the maid's room and the attics, and still further to the left was the door of the room occupied by Jam Singh.

It was a quarter to twelve. Joseph Reynolds was in his room. He was lying on his bed fully dressed, trying to amuse himself with a technically vile translation of a morally vile French novel.

There came ever so faint a tap upon the door. Reynolds got up and opened it stealthily. Jam Singh slipped quietly into the room.

"I thought I told you not to hang about the landing," said Reynolds angrily. "If we're seen together. . . ."

"Yes, but look at the time," urged the Indian, "a quarter to twelve, and nobody in the house gone to bed yet."

"Lucy, the maid, went up ages ago," said Reynolds.

"How do you know?"

"Mrs. Armitage told me. Mrs. Armitage sent her to bed at half-past eight, as soon as she'd finished washing up the dinner things. She's had the sack to-day. Mrs. A. said she'd looked so bad, she was afraid the girl was going to be ill."

"Well then, Miss Snell?" Jam Singh asked.

"She'll be up in a minute. I left her downstairs a quarter of an hour ago. She said she was going to finish a chapter of her book."

"But Mrs. Armitage?"

"She's sure to follow Miss Snell immediately."

"And what about that chap Bromilow and Miss Sylvia?"

"They'll be in any minute," Reynolds replied. "Bromilow promised Mrs. Armitage. They're sure to be in."

"But if they're not?"

"We've safeguarded ourselves, haven't we? The taxi will keep cruising round until you give the all-clear signal from your window."

"Then three hoots on the horn," said Jam Singh. "We did arrange three hoots on the horn, did we not?"

"Yes," assented Reynolds. "Then you go down and let him in. I thought I'd explained that carefully enough before."

"Yes, but if anything should go wrong?"

"Don't go frightening yourself, Jam Singh. Deal with your difficulties when they arrive. There's such a thing as over-precaution. Now you clear, and don't stir out of your room until you hear the three hoots from the taxi."

Jam Singh turned towards the door. Then he suddenly turned and said calmly:

"I saw the housemaid Lucy in the hall this afternoon. She was very much upset. She had been talking with you alone."

"Well, what if she had?" Reynolds asked, abruptly.

Concealing any anxiety he might have been feeling, Jam Singh spoke very quietly, but there was a very grim note in his voice.

"You know our rule. No women to enter into our work."

"Of course I know the rule and I've

stuck to it. The matter between Lucy and me had nothing to do with *our* business. Mrs. A. had just dismissed her, and she was asking me to help her, nothing more."

"Ah! I see."

"You believe?"

"But, of course," Jam Singh answered blandly; "you would not be so foolish as to deceive us."

So Jam Singh was taking up a threatening attitude. Reynolds thought that attack would be the best form of defence. Always carry the war into the enemy's country!

"Deceive you?" he laughed. "If you ask me, the boot's on the other foot! I was not at all satisfied the last time that some of the stuff hadn't been tampered with."

There was an ugly, sinister expression on the Indian's face, as he replied:

"Take care, Mr. Reynolds, you are making very unpleasant suggestions."

"I can't help that," bluffed Reynolds. "You know perfectly well that considerable difficulties were placed in the way of my being able to check the amounts of the stuff."

"It was none of my doing," Jam Singh asserted. "I made no difficulties."

"Possibly not. But someone did and it's not going to happen again, if I can help it. If I catch you or anyone else monkeying about I shall take steps, and pretty drastic steps, too!"

"Are you threatening me with violence?" There was something far more menacing in the deadly calm of Jam Singh than in Reynold's open bullying.

"Never mind about that. I'm just telling you, that's all. Who's coming with the stuff this time? I hope this compatriot of yours is a better man than the one before, whoever he is."

"He is reliable, so I am informed," Jam Singh answered.

"Well, you've told me the amount of the stuff he's supposed to bring. I've got the figures. Now you just get back to your room and keep your ears pricked up for that taxi."

Jam Singh paused a moment before he went to his own room, and said in his blandest possible manner: "Perhaps you would be interested to know what happened to the last member of our organization who was careless about guarding his secret. They cut out his tongue, and sent it to his fiancée." He glided quietly out.

"Wouldn't trust one of them further than I could kick 'em," murmured Reynolds. And then he wondered could he trust Mrs. A. Mrs. A.—dear old Rosie! She was always temperamental and horribly superstitious. How she used to "get the wind up" in the

old days, if someone whistled or quoted
Macbeth in the dressing-room! Why the
devil should it be unlucky to whistle or
quote *Macbeth* in a dressing-room? Still,
there it was. Women are women, and if
they happen to be actresses they're worse
than women, or rather they're women at
their worst, and nothing could be worse than
that. He'd had an example that afternoon
in Lucy. Rosie always had been inquisitive.
She had been in one of her old moods to-day,
she was sure everything was going to go all
wrong, just as she used to be on "first-
nights." He hoped she wasn't going to
"sit up," to see what happened. She had
agreed never to inquire into the nature of
his "activities" so long as he kept his part
of the bargain. But time and again he had
experienced the greatest difficulty in sub-
duing her damned curiosity. Perhaps he had
better go and see if she were in a more
tranquil mood than she had been that afternoon. He went out on to the landing, just
as Mrs. A.—"Rosie"—was coming upstairs
to bed.

Mrs. Armitage stifled a scream. She was,
no doubt, in "one of her old moods," and
the sudden sight of Reynolds was too much
for her.

"Steady on, Rosie, steady on!" he said.
"Where's Miss Snell?"

"What a start you gave me . . . she'll be up directly."

"Pull yourself together, Rosie."

"Oh, Joe . . . !"

"Don't be silly!   Why aren't Sylvia and that young man in yet?"

"How should I know?   They're just a bit late, that's all. Young people out together."

"They're a couple of blasted young nuisances!" he growled.

"That Mr. Bromilow's reliable enough. They'll be in before midnight."

"I should hope so!" he said devoutly. "Anyway, when they *do* come in, call out to Sylvia and pack her off to bed; don't let 'em dawdle about spooning and chattering."

"Of course I shan't allow that, Joe. What d'you think I am?"

"Well, when you've got those two off to bed, go to bed yourself and go to sleep."

"All right."

"And look here, Rosie. If you should happen to hear a bit of movement on the stairs during the night, don't take any notice."

Mrs. Armitage suddenly clutched his arm. "Oh, Joe, I'm so nervous," she exclaimed; "promise me this will be the last time."

"Now, don't let's start all that again," he said irritably.

"I'll have a nervous breakdown soon.   I

hardly know what I'm doing as it is. I'll take the matter into my own hands. You're driving me into a state of desperation, and I'll put an end to these goings on, somehow."

"Oh, you will, will you?" He was once more the overbearing bully. "Now, look here——"

"Hush!" she exclaimed, "here's Miss Snell coming."

"Get her off to bed as quickly as you can!" he almost commanded. And he went back into his room, with a brief "Good night."

Miss Snell came up the stairs with her novel under her arm. She saw Mrs. Armitage.

"I'm quite late to-night!" she said with a giggle; "it's this book. Most absorbing. I've got to *such* a thrilling bit. Elspeth, the heroine, has been driving the young man mad with jealousy, and he suddenly snatches her in his arms and says, 'You tantalising little *devil*, I've a jolly good mind to. . . .'" Sleepiness overcame Miss Snell for the moment, and she yawned, leaving Mrs. Armitage to guess, had she been sufficiently interested, what it was the young man in the novel had a jolly good mind to do.

"Dear me!" exclaimed Miss Snell, "what a sleepy girl I am."

"That's a good thing," said Mrs. Armitage

involuntarily.   Then, recovering herself, "I mean it's a good thing it's Sunday to-morrow.   You'll be able to have a nice, long sleep."

"Yes, indeed," Miss Snell chirruped; "I'm not sure that I shan't be really lazy and have breakfast in bed, if it's not bothering you."

"No bother at all.   Well, good night, Miss Snell."

"Thank you so much.   Good night!" Miss Snell went into her room, then much to Mrs. Armitage's annoyance, suddenly opened the door and looked out again: "Oh, but I was telling you about my book!" she prattled.   "The hero snatches her in his arms and says: 'You tantalizing little *devil*, I've a jolly good mind to . . .'" again Miss Snell yawned, but, at the end of the yawn, con-tinued: "'I've a jolly good mind to . . .' excuse me, I'm afraid I must seem very rude . . . 'I've a jolly good mind to . . . leave you for ever and go to Australia. . . !'"

Mrs. Armitage did not appear to be very much concerned about either the tantalizing little devil, or the gentleman who was con-templating a trip to the Antipodes.

"Of course, I don't know yet whether he actually *does* go to Australia or not," Miss Snell rambled on; "but, in any case, he comes back on the last page.   Either he comes back or she goes there because she's in his arms, and she knows that although she has played with him for two hundred pages she's wanted him all the time in italics. So either she's gone to him, or he's come back to her. I couldn't resist looking at the last page to find out.''

"Quite," said Mrs. Armitage; "well, good night, Miss Snell.''

"Good night, Mrs. Armitage.'' Miss Snell once more vanished into her bedroom, but within a few seconds, she suddenly popped out again.

"You know, Mrs. Armitage," she said dreamily, "Australia must be such a romantic place. Fancy knowing it was really night-time all day. And all those splendid men. And the kangaroos and emus in the desert, and even if they are mainly descended from convicts they did their bit nobly in the war. Fancy the miles and miles of prairie, and the blazing sun burning down on . . . oh, that reminds me, did you put my hot milk in my room? You did? Oh, thank you *so* much. Well, I'm off to the Land of Nod! Good-night, Mrs. Armitage.''

Miss Snell went into her room. Mrs. Armitage descended the stairs to her own.

*   *   *   *   *   *

In her tiny room above, Lucy Timson had lain in a huddled heap on the bed, in the last extremity of despair and misery. All hope had left her. There had only remained the craving for revenge. One man's hideous, cruel selfishness had robbed her of her sanity. She had lain there deserted, unheeded, utterly alone in her agony, deliberately goading herself into the frenzy in which she was to commit a tragic and terrible sin. For a long time the room had echoed with her sobs; but now, at midnight, all was still.

Jam Singh, a little later, was startled to hear a taxi in the street below. Surely the fools hadn't come yet? It was too soon, far too soon. However, he would not give the "all clear" signal until he was sure everyone had gone to bed. His electric torch—was it working all right? Yes. He left it under his pillow, stole to the window, and peered down into the moonlit street.

The taxi stopped outside the door of No. 92. Hugh Bromilow alighted from the taxi and helped Sylvia out. She ran to the door, while Hugh paid the driver. Well, thought Jam Singh, those two would soon be accounted for now.

Hugh and Sylvia had returned from their outing on the best of terms with themselves and with each other. The fact that

Sylvia rather reputed her mother to be "terse" because they were a bit late rather added to the enjoyment of the moment. It was rather fun to feel like naughty children. . . .

*   *   *   *   *   *

"I say, have you enjoyed it?" Hugh asked.

"Rather!" Sylvia answered.

"You haven't been bored?"

"Not a scrap. What do we do next? Say good night and go bye-byes like good children?"

"Not just yet."

"Well, I think that's rather cheek of you. Making me do and say things——"

"The night is still young, Sylvia, and so are we."

"Now I suppose you're going to come over all romantic."

"It's quite probable. I can feel it coming on."

"You don't expect *me* to, do you?"

"I shouldn't be surprised."

"Oh, wouldn't you? I wonder what you're going to make me say next."

"Wait and see. You mustn't butt in, you must let me do as I like. In the meantime, I'm going up on to the landing of the second floor."

"Why?"

"Because it's flooded with moonlight, and moonlight fits in with my mood."

"Well, off you go, then. Good night, Mr. Bromilow, and thank you very much for the pleasant afternoon and evening."

"Good night, Miss Armitage, and thank *you* for the pleasure of your society."

* * * * * *

Hugh got as far as the landing of the first floor. The gas on the second floor was still burning. He remembered Mrs. Armitage's inflexible rule "Last in, turn out the gas." He assumed that he and Sylvia were probably the "last in." He made a move to ascend the next flight of stairs, and then he remembered about his timidity with gas stoves, and rings . . . he did not mind ordinary gas-jets really . . . but . . . if Sylvia came up to turn the gas off. . . .

He looked over the banisters. Sylvia was still in the hall.

"I say!" he said quietly. "This gas is still on. Oughtn't it to be turned off?"

"Will you do it, please," said Sylvia.

"I say," he pleaded, "I'm always such a fool at turning off the gas, I get confused over the taps. Will you come and do it?"

"Oh, dear, *what* a business! Of course I will, silly!"

Sylvia ran quickly up the stairs, past Hugh, and went on to the second landing. She managed the difficult and dangerous feat of turning it off quite adroitly, then stood in the moonlight, leaning over the banisters and looking down at Hugh.

She made a very sweet picture as she stood there. Any member of her own sex would have noticed how well the moonlight showed off her full-skirted georgette frock of cyclamen pink, and silver lamé coat.

"You do look romantic in the moonlight," she said.

"I feel romantic," Hugh replied.

"What a lovely moon! D'you believe it's unlucky to look at it through glass?"

"It depends who you are with. . . ."

"There *is* something funny about the moon, isn't there?"

Sylvia was succumbing to its spell.

"Yes, isn't there? D'you know you look like Juliet at her balcony."

"What nonsense you do talk."

Hugh struck an attitude, and commenced to recite:

"It is the East, and Juliet is the Sun.
  Arise, fair sun, and kill the envious Moon
  That is already sick and pale with grief
  That thou, her maid, and far more fair than she. . . ."

"Good old Shakespeare, he certainly knew a thing or two!"

"Yes," Sylvia agreed; "you do come across some nice bits occasionally." As she spoke she leaned on the banister rail, her cheek in her hand.

"O that I were a glove upon that hand, that I might touch that cheek!" quoted Hugh.

"Well, really, I must say——!"

Hugh continued: "She speaks! O speak again, bright angel!"

"*Sylvia!*" called Mrs. Armitage sharply, from the floor below.

"I come anon!" called Hugh.

"What *are* you talking about?" asked Sylvia, laughing.

"It was most appropriate. That's what Juliet says when the nurse calls to her to come in from the balcony."

"Oh, I see!"

"*Syl-vi-a!*" called Mrs. Armitage again.

"Oh, damn!" said Sylvia.

"Yes," said Hugh; "that's probably more like what Juliet would have really said."

"I must go down and speak to her for a moment." Sylvia came down on to the landing where Hugh stood.

"Come back and say good night, will you?"

"Well—do you think I ought——?"

"Please. Just for a second—please!" he pleaded.

"Righty-ho, I'll be back in a jiffy," and Sylvia ran downstairs to placate her mother.

In the meantime Reynolds, in his room, was saying several unprintable things about lovers and moonlight and Shakespeare in very lurid English. And Jam Singh, also listening impatiently, was muttering still worse things about the same subjects in Hindustani.

Soon Sylvia rejoined Hugh on the landing.

"I say, mother's in rather a wax," she said. "I knew she'd say we ought to have been in earlier. I don't think she really meant it. She always thinks she ought to do the conventional, heavy stuff."

"That's a relief."

"Still, we must say good night."

"I suppose we must!"

"It's high time." Sylvia suddenly started. "What was that?" she asked.

"What?"

"I thought I heard a door opening."

"That's nothing," said Hugh. "This house is full of creaks at night."

"Yes, it is," Sylvia shivered slightly. Hugh drew a little closer to her. "And it's so dark and gloomy. Quite sort of mysterious sometimes, haven't you noticed it?"

"Not particularly"—he slipped his arm around her—"it seems rather nice to me to-night."

"It's different with you here," she said softly.

"What a nice thing to say."

"I meant it."

"Sylvia, dear . . ." Hugh was about to kiss her.

"No, you mustn't!" she urged.

"Why not?"

"You don't really care enough."

"I do, you know I do. I've been trying to tell you all day."

"It's just the effect of the moonlight," she said.

Now, at last, his self-distrust had been swept away.

"I swear it isn't," he said, holding her to him. "I've been crazy about you from the first moment I saw you. Don't you believe me?"

"Oh, I want to believe you, but it's so difficult to be certain of people in these days. Nobody seems to take anything seriously. If only there was some way of making sure!"

If only he could make her feel sure! As sure as he felt himself.

"What can I do to convince you? Sylvia, dearest, I'd do anything in the world."

"Would you?"

"Perhaps something will happen. Some moment may arrive when I can prove to

you how much I care.   In the meantime
. . . ."

"Yes?"

"Tell me you like me a little bit."

"More than a little bit."

"And do you think you would—er—
could—enough to marry me?"

"Perhaps.   You must give me a little
more time.   What was . . . ?"

There was ever such a faint sound behind
them They both swung sharply round.   On
the second floor above them, just at the foot
of the stairs to the attic, stood Lucy Timson, motionless as a statue.   There was something queer and uncanny in the sight.   The
girl still wore her black dress and white
apron, but a shawl was wrapped around her
head.   Some instinct, of decency, perhaps, or
was it some indescribable terror?—kept both
Hugh and Sylvia silent.   The girl looked
steadily in their direction for a few moments,
and then moved deliberately across the
landing and entered Reynolds's room.

Sylvia moved away from Hugh, her head
averted.

"Lucy . . . !" she exclaimed, horrified.
"Oh, Hugh, I wish I hadn't seen that!"

"Perhaps it doesn't mean. . . ."

Sylvia shuddered slightly.   That anything
so ugly, so sordid, should have happened
just when Hugh. . . .

"It was most extraordinary," mused Hugh. "She certainly saw us, and she didn't seem to care a bit about us seeing her."

"It's spoilt our evening."

"Don't think of it like that," he begged her.

"I can't help it. I suppose I ought to go and tell mother, but I'm not going to."

"It's wiser to say nothing about it yet," he agreed.

"Perhaps in the morning. Good night . . . and thank you so much. . . . Good night . . . oh, how beastly . . . !"

Without giving him the final kiss he had hoped for, Sylvia hurried downstairs to her room. It was the first time in her life she had ever come up against anything shameful, and her distress was obvious. Hugh felt profoundly sorry for her, as he gazed after her. Then he went slowly into his room.

Less than a minute later three hoots of a motor horn were heard from the street below. Jam Singh emerged from his room, and glided ever so silently and swiftly down the stairs. Then just as silently, Lucy, her head still muffled with the shawl, came out of Reynolds's room. She closed the door and locked it. Then, taking the key with her, she went quietly up the attic stairs towards her own room. Then up the stairs came Jam Singh. With him was another Indian. Between them they carried a long, rect-

angular box, shaped rather like a coffin.
They carried it stealthily into Jam Singh's
room. Then they both came out. Jam Singh
pointed to the door of Reynolds's room, and
whispered a few words in Hindustani.

    *   *   *   *   *   *

The hours went by, and the landing of
the second floor was bathed in sunlight.
Mrs. Armitage was extremely worried. That
sly little cat Lucy had had her revenge.
Cleared away in the night, apparently, and
left her in the lurch! Mrs. Armitage had
come downstairs as usual, at about half-
past seven, but Lucy was nowhere to be
found. Then she had gone up to the girl's
room to rouse her, and found it empty. She
went and called Sylvia, and the latter had
risen hurriedly to prepare the breakfasts for
the boarders. Having seen that this matter
was well in hand, Mrs. Armitage thought it
wiser to go up and inform her clients of the
state of affairs. She went first to Miss
Snell's room and knocked and called several
times. There was no answer. At last she
opened the door and went into Miss Snell's
room. That, too, was empty.

"Well, I never!" she exclaimed. She
stood for a moment in complete bewilderment, then she went and knocked on Jam
Singh's door.

"Mr. Singh," she called; "Mr. Singh! I'm

sorry you've not been called, but you see, Lucy. . . .   Mr. Singh! *Mr. Singh!*"

There was something very unusual in the air this morning. She looked into the room. Jam Singh was not there.   "Heavens above!" she murmured. "What on earth's happened to the house?"   She went to Reynolds's door.   She was growing more and more alarmed.   She knocked and called repeatedly, "Mr. Reynolds . . . Mr. Reynolds . . . *Mr. Reynolds!*"

Hugh Bromilow came out on to the landing below.

"Hullo, Mrs. Armitage, good morning," he called up to her.   "I say, I've been ringing and ringing."

"Yes, I daresay you have!" she said impatiently.

"And I've had no shaving water or tea."

"I'm very sorry, but the whole house has gone topsy-turvy this morning.   Lucy's gone."

"Gone!   Why?"

"Don't ask me!   When I got up she was nowhere to be seen, and when I went up to her room, thinking she had overslept, it was empty."

"Good Lord!"

"I gave her notice yesterday, and I suppose she's cleared out and left me in the lurch, the little hussy!   But that's not all.

Neither Miss Snell nor Mr. Singh are in their rooms either."

"Good Heavens, an elopement!" exclaimed Hugh.

"It's most extraordinary. Miss Snell said she was going to have breakfast in bed, and Mr. Singh never gets up early on a Sunday."

"I expect they're both at Gretna Green by now," laughed Hugh.

"No, really, I'm worried, Mr. Bromilow. I can tell you it was quite a relief to find that you were still here. I can't get any answer from Mr. Reynolds."

"You were knocking loudly enough, Lord knows."

"Supposing he's gone, too?"

"I should look and see if I were you."

Mrs. Armitage tried to open the door. "It's locked!" she cried. She was becoming thoroughly agitated. She battered on the door impatiently. "Mr. Reynolds! Mr. Reynolds! Oh, dear, *everyone's* gone . . . Mr. Reynolds!"

"Haven't you got another key for his door?" asked Hugh.

"All the locks on this landing are the same."

"Oh, then, that's quite simple," Hugh went to Miss Snell's door and took the key from the lock.

"It's probably locked from the inside," said Mrs. Armitage.

"Well, you can find out by trying this one," said Hugh, giving her Miss Snell's key.

Mrs. Armitage inserted the key in the door of Reynolds's room.

"It fits all right," she said. Then, with an exclamation of relief, she succeeded in unlocking the door. She was about to look into the room, when a sudden thought occurred to Hugh.

"I say, Mrs. Armitage, I suppose—er—Sylvia—er—Miss Armitage is here all right?"

"Yes, I went and called her as soon as I found Lucy had gone. She's downstairs, helping with the breakfasts."

"Well, that's something to be thankful for," said Hugh. He turned and went back into his own room.

A harrowing scream rang through the house. Another, and yet another.

Hugh came out from his room and ran swiftly up the stairs. The door of Reynolds's room was open. Mrs. Armitage came rushing out, still screaming horribly.

"Joe! Joe!" she wailed. "Oh, my God, don't look like that. It's true! Joe! Joe!"

"What is it?" asked Hugh, hurrying to her side.

"*Murder!*"

"Nonsense."

Mrs. Armitage sank into a chair. She pointed feebly at Reynolds's room, then fainted dead away.

Hugh went and looked into the room. Someone had thrown a bright red shawl, or cloak or something loosely over the figure in the bed . . . no, it wasn't a shawl, or a cloak. . . .

He went into the room, nerving himself to look. A hand that seemed made of wax was stretched out towards him, as if trying to ward something off. The arm seemed to emerge somehow from a mass of vivid, hideous crimson. Under the bed there was a dark, gruesome wet patch where the blood had dripped through the mattress, while from the throat of that figure thin strands of crimson curved and drooped as if still spurting out like finest threads of hardened sealing-wax, or the "feelers" of a lobster. It was a sickening, loathsome sight. And from the repellent mass of congealed blood that hid the dead man's throat, there projected, transfixed, a common carving-knife, while two glazed, sightless eyes looked at Hugh with the astonished, angry, pitiful expression of a child that had just received an unexpected blow.

Hugh recovered his self-possession, and went slowly out of the room.

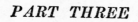

PART THREE

PART THREE

SYLVIA had heard her mother's screams, and come running up the stairs. "Get some brandy," Hugh called to her over the banisters.

"What is it?" she asked breathlessly.

"Your mother's fainted. Can you bring some brandy quickly?"

"Right," said Sylvia. Very soon she came running up on to the landing with the brandy. "What is it? Oh, Hugh, what is it?"

She bent over her mother, and managed to get some brandy between her lips. Mrs. Armitage moaned faintly.

"It's all right, dear," said Hugh, gently. "She's had a bit of a shock, that's all. She's coming round."

"Yes; but what was it?"

"You must be prepared for a shock, dear."

"What?"

"Something rather terrible has happened . . . in there."

"Mr. Reynolds?"

Hugh nodded.

"Dead?"

"Yes, dead. And I'm afraid murdered."

"*Murdered?*"

"I can see no other explanation."

Sylvia began to tremble violently. She turned very white, and her lip began to quiver.

"Oh, how . . . how awful!"

Hugh comforted her as best he could. "Try not to lose your nerve, dear," he urged her; "we'll see this through together. There's usually a policeman at the corner. I'll fetch him at once if he's there. Now, listen, you won't be frightened if I leave you here alone with your mother?"

"No, I won't."

"Sure?"

"Quite sure, Hugh."

He hurried away. Mrs. Armitage was regaining consciousness. Sylvia soothed and coaxed her. She gazed in a terrified manner at the door of that awful room.

"It was a dream, wasn't it . . . what I saw in there . . . a dream, wasn't it?"

"Mother, darling, you must be brave."

"Blood everywhere," moaned Mrs. Armitage; "and that great knife sticking in his throat. Blood . . . and that awful look on his face . . . all surprised."

"Hush, don't think of it," Sylvia pleaded.

"I shall think of it to my dying day
. . . Why can't you tell me it isn't true?"
She tried to rise from the chair; "I'm going
to look again."

"No, mother, no!" Sylvia commanded,
restraining her.

"Then it *is* true! Oh, my God, that it
should end like this! . . . We shall be
ruined, all of us!"

Recovered from the stupefaction the news
of the murder had caused, Sylvia was beginning to wonder at her mother's acute
distress.

"We couldn't help a thing like this
happening," she said.

"Oh, you don't know . . . you don't
know!"

What on earth could her mother mean?
"Mother, you must pull yourself together.
Mr. Bromilow has gone to fetch the police."

"*The police!*" Mrs. Armitage was un-
reasonably alarmed.

The door closed in the hall below.

"They're coming now," said Sylvia.

"But they can't come! Keep them away.
For God's sake! keep them away."

To Sylvia's utter bewilderment, her
mother was quite panic-stricken.

"But they can't come!" she babbled.
"Keep them away—keep them away, for
God's sake! In vain Sylvia tried to quiet

her. "Sylvia, darling, if you love me, don't
let them in yet . . . you don't understand!"

Sylvia most certainly did not understand.

A policeman appeared, coming up the
stairs, followed by Hugh. Mrs. Armitage
was now quite frantic.

"I didn't do it, I swear I didn't!" she
screamed. "It couldn't have been anybody
in this house—there's nothing wrong with
this house."

"Which room?" asked the constable,
ignoring her.

"Straight ahead," said Hugh. The constable entered the room. Hugh turned to
Mrs. Armitage.

"Now, look here, Mrs. Armitage, you
have got to control yourself. Do you
understand?"

"I tell you I didn't. . . ."

"Of course you didn't; but you mustn't
let go of yourself, for your own sake."

"But. . . ."

"Quiet!" he commanded. The constable
came back on to the landing. "Well,
there's no doubt about that!" he remarked
calmly.

"None," agreed Hugh.

"Got a telephone here?"

"Yes, downstairs, just inside the sitting-
room."

"I'll get the Inspector along. You wait

here, if you don't mind." The constable
went downstairs. Mrs. Armitage's behaviour
continued to be both troublesome and
ridiculous, quite inexcusable. At least, so
it appeared to Hugh. Sylvia was beginning
to wonder.

"He suspects me, I know it."

"Be reasonable, mother, how could he?"

"Oh, it's easy enough for you. . . ."

"It isn't particularly pleasant for any of
us, mother."

"The policeman's coming back again now.
He'll be asking all sorts of questions."

"Well, you must answer them as well as
you can," said Hugh.

"You've nothing to fear, Mummy."

"Oh, haven't I?"

"No, no—we'll stick by you. Won't we,
Sylvia?"

"Rather."

The constable rejoined them, notebook
in hand. "And now," said he, "I'll take
a few particulars if you don't mind, while
we're waiting for the Inspector. Now,
first of all, who's the occupier of the
house?"

"This lady here is the landlady," said
Hugh.

"And your name, madam?"

Mrs. Armitage suddenly realized that she
was in the limelight, as it were, and this

calmed her considerably. In the old days she had always had hysterics on first nights, and declared she couldn't "go on." But once the show started she gradually got the better of her nerves."

"Rosabel Ivy Armitage."

"And you are the occupier."

"The lease of the house is in my name." Yes; she was feeling better now. Quite important, in fact. The policeman, no doubt, admired her for her *sangfroid* and common-sense.

"Married or single?"

"Married."

"Your husband here?"

"No."

"I see, living apart."

That set her off again. "There you are, I told you he'd start suggesting things."

"Hush, mother, he didn't quite understand. My father is away for the night at Brighton. He'll be back during the morning."

"Oh, I see . . . beg pardon, no offence meant. You, then, are Miss Armitage—if it is Miss."

"Only for the time being," said Hugh.

"You live here at home."

"Yes," Sylvia answered. "I assist in the running of the house. We have lodgers here, you see."

"Oh, lodgers! The deceased was a lodger?"

"Yes."

"How long had he been here?"

"Well, my mother would. . . ."

"He's been here a considerable time off and on," said Mrs. Armitage. "I should say about ten years."

"What was his name?"

"Joseph Reynolds."

"Any relations that you know of?"

"No . . . we know nothing about his private life, nothing at all." Mrs. Armitage was growing apprehensive again.

"Still, in ten years you'd get to know him fairly well."

"Only fairly well."

"D'you know if he possessed any enemies?"

"None to my knowledge."

"Then, what is more important, do you know if he had any peculiar attachments?"

"How do you mean?" She was obviously nervous again.

"Well, is there any lady who . . . ?"

"No . . . well . . . no."

"Are you sure?"

"Yes . . . I mean . . . cf course . . . I . . ." Mrs. Armitage rapidly became quite hysterical. "I . . . what are you staring at me like that for? . . . I can't bear it. . . . Oh! . . . I've told you all I know . . . !" The poor woman completely lost her self-control and relapsed into hysterical cries and laughter.

"I'll take her in here for a little while till she recovers," said Sylvia, and she led her mother into Miss Snell's room.

"She'll have to see the Inspector, you know, when he arrives," continued the constable. "Now, sir, can I have *your* name?"

"Hugh Bromilow."

"You are a lodger here?"

"Yes."

"How long have you been here?"

"About three months."

"Occupation?"

"Oh well . . . I write."

"Write?" The constable was somewhat at a loss.

"Yes; stories and things. Stories mostly."

"Ah," assented the constable; "but how do you earn your living?"

"Just by my writing," Hugh answered, concealing his amusement. "Editors pay me something from time to time."

"H'm . . . casual employment," commented the constable, duly making a note of it in his book.

The bell rang.

"The Inspector," said the constable. As he went downstairs Sylvia came out of Miss Snell's bedroom.

"She's quieter now," Sylvia said. "Where's the policeman?"

"Gone downstairs to let the Inspector in."

"Hugh, it's all too dreadful. There's so much I can't understand. Mother's behaviour——"

"She's suffering from shock, quite naturally."

"No, it's more than that, she knows things. What are we to do? I feel so helpless."

"Listen, dear." Hugh placed his hands on her shoulders, and spoke tenderly. His manner was reassuring, protective. "You remember last night, how I said that some moment might arrive when I could prove to you how much. . . . Well, don't you see, the moment has come. Whatever happens I'm going to help you, and I promise you if there is anything on earth I can do, I'll star d between you and this horrible affair. Now, look here, I'm going to have a little private reconnoitre on my own account."

"Oh, Hugh, be careful."

"Which is Lucy's room?"

"The one on the left."

Hugh ran up the stairs to Lucy's room. Sylvia joined her mother in Miss Snell's. A moment later the constable arrived on the landing, followed by an Inspector.

"Straight across . . ." said the constable, indicating the room where the murdered man lay.

"You'd better come in too," said the Inspector; "the men downstairs have got their instructions."

Sylvia found her mother much calmer. She did her best to soothe her and give her courage. "After all," she said, "we none of us know anything about it. All we have to do is to answer the questions simply."

"That's right!" her mother assented. "We none of us know anything about it." There was a hint of auto-suggestion in the remark.

"All the others have got to be questioned too, Mummy!"

"But where *are* the others I should like to know?" exclaimed Mrs. Armitage, suddenly seeing them collectively as the murderer of poor Reynolds. "That Mr. Jam Singh—nasty, sneaking heathen! And Miss Snell, for all her old-maidish ways."

"Surely you can't imagine that poor Miss Snell. . . ."

"You never know with these quiet

spinsters. Still waters run deep, that's what I always say. And then, of course, I was forgetting Lucy."

Sylvia suddenly, and for the first time, recalled the untoward incident that had occurred the previous night.

"Oh, Lucy!" she exclaimed.

"Yes—Lucy!" It was Hugh's voice, and he spoke very significantly, as he came down from Lucy's room.

"Heavens, what a shock you gave me," cried Mrs. Armitage.

Sylvia turned to Hugh: "In all this upset I'd forgotten all about last night and Lucy and . . . what we saw."

"I hadn't forgotten," said Hugh.

"What did you see last night, Sylvia?" asked Mrs. Armitage, eagerly.

"We shall tell the police," Sylvia said.

"We shall have to," from Hugh.

"But what did you . . . ?"

"Never mind about that now, Mrs. Armitage," Hugh interrupted. "Tell me, does Lucy smoke cigarettes?"

"Yes; I caught her smoking in the scullery the other day."

"Did Mr. Reynolds smoke?"

"Only his pipe. He detested cigarettes."

"Jam Singh?"

"I don't know."

"I do," broke in Sylvia. "He never

smokes at all. He says it's against his religion, or something."

"Hush!" said Hugh, "they're coming."

Out came the Inspector—brisk, efficient, imperturbable, followed by the constable. He took the constable's notebook and referred to it, as he conducted his own examination without any loss of time. This, then, was Mrs. Armitage, the young lady was her daughter, and the young man one of the lodgers. Mr. Armitage was at Brighton but was expected back shortly. The other lodgers weren't in the house. Well, anyhow, who were the other lodgers? A Mr. Jam Singh, an Indian gentleman, said to be a student.

"Did he sleep here last night?"

"I suppose so. I don't know."

"Which is his room? That one? Have a look, will you?"

This last to the constable, who went into the Indian's room. The Inspector carried on with his examination. The Indian gentleman had been in the house about seven months. Not much known about him. Out all day, said to be at some college. Kept himself to himself.

The constable rejoined the others. "The bed's not slept in," he reported.

"Who's the other lodger?" inquired the Inspector.

"A Miss Snell," replied Mrs. Armitage; "a maiden lady she is. Always seemed very nice and refined, but still. . . ."

"And she's out too—is that usual?"

"Not at all. Especially as her last words to me last night were that she was going to have breakfast in bed."

"Both Mr. Singh and Miss Snell have latchkeys?"

"Yes."

"Go downstairs and tell the men guarding the hall they're to keep out of sight. If these two people return, they'll try to do a bolt if they've anything to do with this, and catch sight of the police. Tell the men not to show themselves. They're to allow anyone with a latchkey to come right in, as they would in the ordinary course of events. Same applies to the men in the basement. Nobody is to leave the house under any circumstances whatsoever."

The constable went below. The Inspector proceeded:

"How many servants have you?"

"My daughter and I do nearly all the work, so we only have one servant. At least we *had* one."

"What?" exclaimed the Inspector, showing for the first time some signs of excitement, "has she disappeared too?"

"Yes."

"What was her name?"

"Lucy. Lucy Timson."

"When did she go?"

"During the night, as far as I can make out. She went to bed very early. Half-past eight. She'd got a very bad headache. She'd been—she'd been crying a lot. I'd given her notice yesterday afternoon."

"For any particular reason?"

"Reason!" Mrs. Armitage suddenly flared up "Dozens of reasons! The trouble that girl's been to me . . . smashing things every day, distasteful, bone lazy . . . carrying on with every Tom, Dick and Harry of a tradesman's boy! Quite apart from that——"

"I see!" cut in the Inspector, "generally unsatisfactory."

"If you like to put it that way. *I* would express it quite differently!"

"You have already," rejoined the Inspector. "Now, you discovered that this Lucy Timson had gone—when? This morning?"

"Yes; when I went down to the kitchen she wasn't to be found. Then I went to her room and found it empty. Later on I came up to ask the boarders to excuse the muddle this morning."

"And you found Mr. Singh and Miss Snell

not in their rooms, and then you found the deceased, Mr.—Mr.—Reynolds?"

"I shall never forget it. I can't get the sight out of my mind. There he was with blood all . . ."

"The door was locked?"

Mrs. Armitage covered her face with her hands and shuddered. Hugh interposed and told the Inspector how he had come out on to the landing when Mrs. Armitage was knocking on Reynolds's door, which was locked. He described how the door had been opened with a key from Miss Snell's door. The Inspector duly noted that all the locks in the bedroom doors were the same. "Have you any idea what time the murdered man went to bed last night?" he questioned.

"Well, yes," said Mrs. Armitage; "about a quarter to twelve."

"How do you know?"

"He said good night to me here on this landing at that time."

"You were, apart from the person who committed the crime, the last person to see Joseph Reynolds alive?"

"Yes, I suppose so."

"And that was at 11.45 p.m.?"

"I think so. It was just before Sylvia and Mr. Bromilow came in."

Here the constable returned and told the Inspector that the men below understood their instructions. No one was to leave the house, and anyone with a latchkey would come straight in, in the ordinary way.

"Miss Armitage and I came in at ten to twelve," said Hugh. "I remember looking at my watch, because we were rather later than we intended."

"Now, Mrs. Armitage, the last you saw of the maid, Lucy Timson, was when you sent her to bed at half-past eight?"

"That was the last I saw of her."

"Between half-past eight and a quarter to twelve, she could, I suppose, have cleared out of the house without you or anyone else knowing about it?"

"She could have," Mrs. Armitage assented.

"But she didn't," declared Hugh.

"Oh!" the Inspector scarcely showed any interest.

"Lucy was still in the house at midnight, because Miss Armitage and I saw her," Hugh continued.

"I should like particulars of that, please."

"Well, Miss Armitage and I were having a little final . . . er . . . er . . . conversation together on the lower landing there, when the sound of someone on those stairs" —he indicated the flight that led to Lucy's room and the attics—"attracted our attention. We looked round and there was Lucy at the foot of the stairs watching us."

"Did you speak to her," asked the Inspector.

"No, as a matter of fact we were rather startled."

"Why?"

"She was wearing a shawl over her head, and she looked slightly . . . well . . . ominous, standing there. She stood for a moment or so staring in our direction, and then she walked deliberately to Mr. Reynolds's door, opened it and went in."

Mrs. Armitage was furious. "She went into his room?" she cried. "Why didn't you tell me at once, Miss Sylvia?"

Hugh answered calmly: "We didn't think it wise to mention it just then, Mrs. Armitage."

"Not wise, indeed! I'd have turned the little slut out of the house there and then!"

"That was just the point, mother," interposed Sylvia; "we felt that a scene at that time of night would have been worse than what had already happened."

"I always knew she was a vile . . ."

The Inspector cut short Mrs. Armitage's tirade. "Just one moment, please. Now, sir, after the maid had gone into his room, what did you do?"

"We said good night hurriedly, and went to our respective rooms," Hugh replied.

"You heard no sounds during the night?"

"I went to sleep at once; I was tired," said Sylvia.

"And you, sir?"

"I didn't go to sleep at once, but I heard nothing."

"You ought to have told me, Sylvia."

"I was going to mention it in the morning, mother."

"All this terrible business might have been avoided. The little devil!"

The Inspector proceeded with his questions.

"You think Lucy saw you?"

"I'm quite certain she did. Aren't you, Sylvia?"

"Quite certain."

"That was the peculiar part of it," Hugh declared; "we were standing in the strong moonlight, we must have been particularly distinct against the window, and she was staring straight in our direction. She couldn't have failed to see us, and yet she made no attempt to conceal her actions. It was almost as if she *wanted* us to see what she was going to do."

"The brazen little slut!" ejaculated Mrs. Armitage.

"I'd better have a detailed description of her and have it circulated at once," said the Inspector. "Also of the other two lodgers in case——"

The hall door banged below.

"This is one of 'em," he said. The constable made a move towards the stairs. "No; let 'em come right up," said the Inspector, "whoever it is."

Everyone stood clear of the banisters, so as not to be seen. The constable stationed himself in front of Miss Snell's door, as that lady herself came running up the stairs. She came up rapidly, with a kind of air of grim, blind determination. She might either have been terrified, or in a desperate hurry to get somewhere. There was something indescribably funny in the sight. Miss Snell saw no one in her excitement, until she was actually on the landing. Only for a second a look of utter bewilderment held her features, the next instant she made a dive towards her room, trying to force her way past the burly constable.

"Just one moment, please," said the Inspector.

Miss Snell looked from one to another of the group, with a look of mute agony, then turned and ran full tilt into the constable, as if she could, by a supreme effort of the will, run straight through him into her room.

But matter triumphed over mind, and the poor lady made no headway.

"I'm afraid I must trouble you for two or three minutes."

Miss Snell merely looked agonized again. Perhaps if she couldn't walk through a policeman she might cause him to remove himself. Perchance a subconscious desire to destroy policemen which, had been left over from the days of the militant suffragettes, nerved her to the effort. At any rate, all timidity had been banished by this grim determination to get into that room. In desperation she began to kick the constable's shins.

"'Ere, 'ere, *'ere!*" he remonstrated.

"It's all right, Miss Snell," said Hugh persuasively; "something rather unfortunate has happened, and this gentleman wants to ask a few questions."

Miss Snell shook her head violently. It was a flat refusal to comply with any such request.

"Now please, miss," began the Inspector, "may I have your name in full?"

There was more obstinacy than agony in her expression now. She kept her mouth shut so tightly it might have been hermetically sealed.

"You will oblige me with **an answer,** miss?"

"Poor dear, she's nervous," Sylvia exclaimed. "You needn't be nervous, Miss Snell; it's just one or two simple questions; it's nothing to worry about. I'm sure you will be able to explain everything satisfactorily."

"We hope so," remarked Mrs. Armitage.

"Now please, miss, I'm waiting." The Inspector spoke very firmly.

Miss Snell was crimson with embarrassment. She looked appallingly self-conscious, but at the same time resentful and sulky. Her demeanour was exactly that of a parrot refusing to "show off" before visitors.

"Perhaps she's ill," Hugh suggested.

"Are you ill?"

Miss Snell shook her head.

"Any impediment in her speech?"

Miss Snell shook her head emphatically and angrily.

"Well, then, surely she can answer a simple question," said the Inspector. "Possibly she doesn't understand the seriousness of the situation. Let me tell you that there's been a murder in this house. Mr. Joseph Reynolds has been stabbed in the throat during the night. He's lying there in that room now."

Miss Snell shrank away from the door. She turned pale and looked utterly shocked and horrified, but still she kept her mouth grimly shut, and made not a sound.

"We want all the information we can get from every member of this household. *Now*, perhaps you will speak."

Silence.

"For the last time, Miss Snell, are you prepared to answer my questions?"

Silence.

"You realize that if you persist in this attitude I shall be compelled to ask you to accompany me to the station?"

"Oh, Miss Snell, please speak up!" begged Sylvia. "What on earth is the matter?"

Miss Snell beckoned to Sylvia.

"I think perhaps she'll explain to me," Sylvia suggested.

"Very well!"

Sylvia went to Miss Snell. A whispered conversation ensued between them.

"Oh, good gracious!" Sylvia exclaimed, in a tone of slightly shocked amusement. She then went to the Inspector, and almost bursting with suppressed mirth, she whispered something in his ear.

"Oh, my Gawd!" he cried.

"May she?" entreated Sylvia.

"Oh, for heaven's sake, yes!" he answered; "let her go into her room, constable."

Miss Snell made a hurried exit from the scene.

"Well, never in all my experience!" exclaimed the astounded Inspector.

"But, please, may we know what was the trouble?" Hugh inquired.

Sylvia's answer was interrupted by suppressed gusts of laughter.

"The poor dear . . . she suddenly decided to go to early service at St. Pancras. Just as she got to the door of the church she found that she'd . . . oh, I can't . . . !" Here Sylvia began to laugh unrestrainedly. "She—she—found that she'd come out and forgotten her teeth."

There was a general explosion of mirth.

"Hush, she'll hear us, poor dear! She rushed back to fetch her teeth, and came scuttling up the stairs to avoid seeing anyone, and having to say good morning."

"Hush!" exclaimed Hugh. "She's coming."

There was an awkward pause. Everyone was suffering from what might be described as a backwash from Miss Snell's recent embarrassment. That is to say, everyone but Miss Snell herself. For as soon as this amazing spinster had fitted her teeth into her face once again, she had completely recovered her self-possession. She advanced on to the landing again with complete *aplomb*, just as if she were making her first appearance on the scene. She smiled expansively at the Inspector, showing two complete rows of white, even teeth, and said with much gentility and charm of manner:

"You wish to speak to me, I believe?"

"What is your name, please?"

"Phœbe Mercia St. John Snell. I omit the Mercia on my visiting cards; it looked too pretentious . . . my dear father always said. . . ."

"At what time did you retire to bed last night?"

"Shortly before midnight. Rather late for me, I'm afraid, but my novel led me astray. Usually, I'm early to bed, early to rise, as the saying goes. A cousin of mine in the Civil Service always told me that. . . ."

"Did you go to sleep at once?"

"As soon as my head touched the pillow," replied Miss Snell, as if she were reciting the first line of a poem. "There was no counting sheep going through a gate for *me*, last night. Not that I ever find that much good. Because sheep don't as a rule, go through a gate one at a time, and I've got such a *vivid* imagination, I always fancy I can hear them 'baa-ing,' and the noise keeps me awake. But thank heaven, I'm not often. . . ."

"You heard nothing during the night or early morning?"

"No, no; I slept very soundly indeed . . .

Oh! wait a moment . . . now I come to think of it . . . I . . . er . . . I . . . er . . . ."

"Yes?"

"I had a particularly vivid dream. I was on a motor-cycling tour in Spain, riding pillion behind the Home Secretary, of all people . . . most unconventional—when suddenly. . . ."

"So you heard nothing at all? And when you woke up you decided to go to church, and—well, the rest of the story we know. Now, can you tell us anything about the deceased?"

"The deceased?" Miss Snell had completely forgotten—so thoroughly was she enjoying being interviewed by a police inspector—what the interview was about.

"Mr. Joseph Reynolds."

"Oh, yes, of course . . . how terrible. No, I'm afraid I can tell you nothing about him. He was a very peculiar man in some ways."

"Peculiar? How?"

"Well, he was quite *unusually* fond of boiled mutton and caper sauce, and . . . well, I only know him—*knew* him very slightly. How dreadful for you, Mrs. Armitage. And you, Miss Sylvia! In such a nice house as this! Appalling!"

"When you went out early this morning,

Miss Snell, did you see anyone on the stairs or in the hall?"

"Not a single soul."

"You didn't see the maid Lucy?"

"No."

"Nor the Indian gentleman, Jam Singh?"

"No, no one at all. Is Mr. Singh not here this morning?"

"He is not."

"How very strange! You don't think that he. . . ."

The hall door banged again.

"This may be him now," said Hugh.

Sylvia leant over the banisters. "Yes. Yes, it is," she whispered.

"Take care, don't let him see you," the Inspector warned her.

Jam Singh came hurrying up the stairs. He reached the landing, then suddenly stood stock still, as if he were turned to stone. The sight of the police seemed to have paralysed him.

"Your name is Jam Singh," said the Inspector sharply; "I want you to answer a few questions."

The Indian burst forth into a panic-stricken, high-pitched volley of protest:

"No! No!" he positively shrieked. "I know nothing . . . nothing. . . . It's nothing to do with me . . . it's a trap! I refuse. . . .!"

He turned and started to rush down the stairs.

"Stop him, Rogers!" shouted the Inspector.

The constable was after Jam Singh like a flash of lightning. He caught him on the lower landing. The Indian fought, bit and kicked and scratched like a mad animal, and a terrific struggle ensued. Suddenly they crashed with terrible force into the slender wooden banisters. There was a sound of rending wood, a scream from Jam Singh, an unrepeatable exclamation from the constable, and a shout of horror from all the onlookers, as both the combatants fell headlong into the depths below.

*   *   *   *   *   *

The constable was unhurt, for he had fallen right on top of the frightened Indian; but it seemed to Hugh, who quickly made an examination, that one of Jam Singh's legs were broken. They carried him into the sitting-room, placed him on a couch, and Hugh and Sylvia extemporized a rough splint for his leg. The terrified fellow was in a state of utter collapse, and apparently unconscious. Miss Snell fussed around with brandy.

"I often think I ought to have taken up

nursing professionally," she rambled. "My chemist in Southampton Row. . . ."

Jam Singh began to show signs of coming round. The Inspector sent the constable with instructions that one of the others should fetch an ambulance or a stretcher. He hadn't any doubt that the fellow could be made to talk after such a shaking up.

"What's happened . . . where am I?" murmured Jam Singh faintly. "Ow . . . my leg . . . !" The impulse to attempt flight for a second time was frustrated.

"I should keep perfectly still if I were you," Hugh advised him. "You've had a most remarkable escape, but I'm very much afraid you've broken your leg."

"It was unwise of you to become so violent, Mr. Singh," said the Inspector. "However, perhaps you'll now oblige me by answering a few questions."

"What questions? I know nothing. I'm perfectly innocent."

"You could hardly expect me to believe that after your behaviour upstairs."

"I was nervous. I'm a foreigner in this country. The police always alarm me . . . I lost my head for a moment. . . ."

The constable returned, and set to work making notes of the conversation.

"Come, come!" said the Inspector: "The matter's far too serious for you to take up that tone. You've put yourself in a very dangerous position, and the sooner you realize it the better."

"I don't understand your meaning."

"Well, then, let me inform you . . . that's if you don't know already—that Mr. Joseph Reynolds has . . ."

Jam Singh uttered a cry of despair: "Reynolds! My God . . . ! You've got him? Where is he? Why isn't he here? You've taken him away . . ."

The Inspector, face to face with some totally unexpected turn in the affair, never turned a hair. He saw his opportunity to bluff, and took it.

"No," he said. "We've not taken him away yet. He's . . . he's upstairs."

"Under arrest?" asked Jam Singh, falling into the trap.

"And why should he be under arrest?"

"So he's double-crossed us!" shouted Jam Singh. "I knew he would, the pig-dog. He's put it all on to me, I see it now."

The bewilderment of the others was intense. Only the faces of the Inspector and the constable remained impassive.

"I'm glad you see it now."

"Very well then," exclaimed Jam Singh, fiercely. "I'll give the whole show away. I'll turn King's evidence—ask me whatever questions you like."

"Then perhaps you'll give an account of your movements last night."

"I stayed in all the evening."

"Where?"

"In my room. Shortly before midnight I went in to see Reynolds, in his room. I began to feel nervous that our plans might go wrong."

"Yes," bluffed the Inspector, "but you'd laid your plans very carefully, hadn't you?"

"Yes; but I'd been losing confidence in Reynolds for some time past. However, after a short discussion we parted."

"And then?"

"Then, when the signal came, I went downstairs as we'd arranged, to fetch the stuff."

"The stuff?"

"The dope."

A murmur of astonishment fell from everyone's lips.

The Inspector said, calmly:

"Yes, of course—the dope."

"Everything went according to plan," Jam Singh continued; "but when I went to Reynolds's room to check the amounts with him, I found the door locked. I tapped as lightly as I could, but got no answer."

"Perhaps he was asleep?"

"That was impossible with our business on hand. It stood to reason he must be very much on the alert. I began to smell a rat . . . all my suspicions that he might be cheating us came to a head . . . I got into a panic. I went back to my room, where I had left my confederate; we packed up the stuff again and hurried off with it straight back to headquarters."

"Ah, yes, of course!" said the Inspector.

"I suppose Reynolds has told you all about headquarters?"

"No, he hasn't. . . ."

"He hasn't?" cried Jam Singh, eagerly: "Well, then, we can come to an understanding . . . I can give you all the information you want, names and everything, and then we can fix things so that I can get off lightly . . . I know these things can be arranged. How much has Reynolds told you?"

Then the Inspector, seeing that the moment had come, suddenly abandoned his bluff.

"Reynolds has told us nothing!" he said, very sharply.

"Nothing? I don't understand."

"Reynolds will never tell anyone anything again."

"You mean . . . he's left the country? But you said he was upstairs."

"Yes; he's upstairs in his room, dead."

"Dead! My God! It can't be. . . ."

"He's been murdered."

"Murdered?"

"He was murdered during the night. We've been here investigating the crime."

"The crime! Dead . . . ? Then you didn't. . . ."

Suddenly the wretched man realized that he had been led into a trap. "Oh, I see now . . . I see what a fool I've been! I spoke too quickly. You knew nothing about our other business?"

"Nevertheless we're very grateful for the information."

"You shall have no more, I promise you that!" vowed Jam Singh.

"We shall see. I think you'll find it necessary to tell us everything."

"You can't be going to accuse me of murder?"

"It doesn't strike me as being impossible."

"But," pleaded the Indian frantically, "surely you realize that I knew nothing—absolutely nothing about the murder? You know why I tried to escape. It was because I thought you were after us for the dope."

The Inspector, reviewing rapidly in his mind the evidence of the others, made a sudden shot in the dark.

"Now, in reference to this dope trafficking. The housemaid, Lucy Timson, was part of the organization, wasn't she?"

"The maid? Certainly not! We never employ women in our work. I had to remind Reynolds of the fact yesterday."

"Oh! Why was that?"

"Because I saw the maid Lucy going out of his room yesterday afternoon. She was very upset, and she'd been in there alone with Reynolds. She was weeping with rage, and I heard her muttering to herself: 'I'll show him, the brute; I'll make him sorry for this'—or words to that effect."

"She appeared resentful then?"

"Furiously resentful."

"Did you form any idea why?"

"It seemed to me there was some sort of intrigue between Reynolds and Lucy."

"Oh, Mr. Singh!" exclaimed Miss Snell suddenly. "I don't think you ought to say a thing like that about a dead man."

"You mind your own business, Miss Snell. You don't know what *we* know about Lucy and her goings on."

"But why not question Lucy?" urged Jam Singh. "She'll be able to tell you more than I." The Indian was very anxious to get Lucy implicated as deeply as possible.

"She's gone," the Inspector told him, watching carefully for the effect of the news; "disappeared during the night."

"Ah, is that so?" exclaimed Singh, with

obvious satisfaction. "And this morning Reynolds is found dead. It does not seem to me that you will have to look very far for your murderer. She was mad with rage. I could see it clearly. She was in a state when she could have done anything."

"Then you don't know," interposed Sylvia, "you don't know what Mr. Bromilow and I saw last night when we came in? We saw Lucy. . . ."

"You needn't tell him that," said the Inspector.

Mrs. Armitage's seething jealousy of the maid was not to be disguised. "It was that girl! I know it was, the little viper!" she exclaimed; "I always knew she was a bad lot!"

The excitement seemed to be revealing more than one repressed emotion. A hitherto carefully disguised antagonism between the landlady and Miss Snell began to manifest itself.

"You mustn't jump to conclusions too easily, Mrs. Armitage," Miss Snell said. "I remember a legal friend of mine who used to say: 'An open mind is far above rubies,' or words to that effect."

"Don't you tell me," snapped Mrs. Armitage. "I *know*. I don't need any legal nonsense."

"I am sure my friend never talked nonsense, Mrs. Armitage. A most highly cultured man . . . the examinations he had to pass!"

"Oh, fiddlesticks!"

"Ladies, please," remonstrated the Inspector.

"Well, really . . . " Miss Snell persisted. "There may have been a murder in the house, but I don't see that's the reason why we should have any *unpleasantness.* As I said: 'An open mind. . . . '"

"Oh, I've no patience with her really"— Mrs. Armitage was really angry now— "everything points to Lucy. It's as plain as the nose on Miss Snell's face, or very nearly as plain!"

In vain Sylvia tried to intervene and restore peace. In vain Hugh remonstrated.

"I won't remain here to be insulted!" Miss Snell cried, doing her utmost to be impressive, and thinking she was succeeding admirably. "Inspector, may I go to my room?"

"By all means."

"Good riddance to bad rubbish," sneered Mrs. Armitage, with more venom than originality.

"I refuse to enter into a vulgar brawl, Mrs. Armitage. I hope I have some sense of dignity. There is much I *could* say."

"Yes, I daresay, now that you've got your teeth in!"

That was really the winning shot of the battle. It "registered," and blew Miss Snell's dignity to smithereens, as it were, though she managed to fight on a bit longer.

"Oh!" Miss Snell's voice rose to an agonized wail. "I shall leave this house as soon as the police allow me."

"Good!" said Mrs. Armitage, definitely.

Miss Snell went to the door, then turned to deliver a final word or two. "I haven't uttered a murmur of complaint of the appalling discomfort I've suffered in this ill-organized house. I shall say nothing of the disgusting food . . . tepid bath water, and the lumpy beds. I shall be thankful to leave here . . . I shall go to a nice *pension* I know of in the South of France. I've finished with Bloomsbury, I'm glad to say! As Tennyson wrote . . . or was it Longfellow . . . ? 'Quoth the raven, never again'!"

Miss Snell went out and slammed the door in a most unladylike manner.

Mrs. Armitage sprang up in a fury. "She's not going to get away with the last word like that. I'll go and have it out with her, here and now." And Mrs. Armitage, too, flounced out of the room.

The Inspector shrugged his shoulders. "Well, I don't mind coping with murder."

All the time Hugh had been steadily thinking things out on his own account.

"Still, Inspector," said he, "there's something in what Miss Snell says about an open mind. . . ."

"H'm, you think so, do you? Well, personally I don't think there's much doubt in this case."

Another constable looked in at the door. "The men have arrived with the stretcher, sir," he announced.

"Tell 'em to come in," he said; then turning to Jam Singh, he added: "We'll get the police-surgeon to fix your leg at the station."

"You going to take me to the police-station?" Jam Singh had flattered himself that now the suspicion seemed to have been definitely removed from him to Lucy, his premature confession about the dope might possibly be overlooked.

"Yes," said the Inspector. "There are some further inquiries we shall have to make."

Jam Singh was rapidly growing frantic with fear again.

"But you won't charge me with murder?"

"We shall see. . . . There's all this dope trafficking to be cleared up."

Two more policemen entered the room with a stretcher.

"You can't charge me with murder!" clamoured Jam Singh, "you *can't!* You *can't!*"

"Here, don't lose your head, Singh," said Hugh, offering his cigarette case. "Have a cigarette."

"No, no! I never smoke at all." The stretcher was lifted. "*Ow*—my leg—— I'll tell you about the other business as long as you don't charge me with murder"—he was now babbling distractedly in his terror— "I'm completely innocent of that . . . it was Lucy——"

They carried Jam Singh downstairs and out of the house. The others in the drawing-room heard his voice rising higher and higher: "Everything points to her, doesn't it. . . . Everything points to Lucy. . . . Everything points to Lucy!"

It seemed as if the whole house were echoing with the words:

"Everything points to Lucy!"

PART FOUR

PART FOUR

ALMOST immediately after the removal of Jam Singh, one of the constables came back into the room and announced that Mr. Armitage had returned home and was talking to his wife in the hall.

"All right, tell him I'll see him later," said the Inspector. "You see," he continued, explaining his attitude to Hugh and Sylvia, "I'm sure that until I told him myself, he hadn't the faintest idea that Reynolds was dead. No; as Jam Singh said, everything points to Lucy quite definitely."

"Almost too definitely," Hugh ventured to observe.

"What do you mean?"

"Well, I can't get over her extraordinary behaviour in making no attempt to conceal things when we saw her last night. When you're going to a man's room to murder him, you don't usually make a point of having two spectators."

"Perhaps when she went in she didn't intend to murder," Sylvia suggested.

"She had that large knife with her, hadn't she?" urged the Inspector. "She must have brought it up with her from the kitchen. Her intentions were pretty clear."

"What isn't clear to me is, why did she deliberately want us to see her?" Hugh insisted.

"The trouble with you, Mr. Bromilow is, that being a writer you're anxious to find a mystery in all this. Believe me, murders aren't often as mysterious as they are in magazine stories, you know, they're much more simple."

"All the same, I don't believe that this case is quite so simple as it looks."

Mrs. Armitage entered the room, followed by her husband.

"Here's the Inspector, Edward. Inspector, this is my husband."

"Good morning," said Mr. Armitage. He was looking a little pale and agitated, but he was keeping remarkably calm for so naturally timid a man. It seemed, when it came to a crisis, Armitage had far more pluck and common-sense than his somewhat overbearing wife.

"Good morning. A rather disturbing home-coming for you, I'm afraid."

"Dreadful—dreadful. Good morning, Mr. Bromilow. Hullo, Sylvia, dear! Nasty upset for you, but you must try not to worry."

"I'm all right, daddy."

"My wife has been telling me everything. I can't realize it all yet. I do hope, Inspector, you realize that my wife and I knew nothing whatever about all this drug trafficking."

"Oh, yes! I think it's pretty evident that you were all duped. You formed a very good screen to their real activities. You were at Brighton all the time, Mr. Armitage?"

"Yes, I stayed the night at an old schoolfriend's."

"Can I have the name and address, please?"

"Of course. Fred Spencer, 39a West Marine Terrace."

"Right."

"I'm afraid, Mr. Bromilow," said Mr. Armitage apologetically, "after all this you'll want to leave here."

"Not at all, I assure you."

The Inspector smiled sarcastically. "Mr. Bromilow's getting what these writer-fellows call 'copy' out of this business. He's busy trying to make a complicated story out of it. He doesn't like the obvious solution."

"It seems to me too obvious," Hugh asserted. "I can't get over the way Lucy went into Reynolds's room."

"We don't have to bother about the way she went in," the Inspector was growing dogmatic; "what concerns us is the fact that she *did* go in. The rest is merely an impression. Impressions will lead you all over the place. Why, you'll be suggesting soon that perhaps it wasn't Lucy at all that you and Miss Armitage saw."

"It was Lucy, without a doubt," Sylvia declared.

"Yes . . . unless . . . I wonder . . . !" murmured Hugh. "Supposing it wasn't?" Hugh began to wander about the room, as was his habit when deep in thought. The Inspector was asking for information about Lucy. No one seemed to have any idea as to where she would go. Sylvia had heard Lucy mention an uncle in Ireland. The Inspector declared that the police would have all the boats watched, and he asked for a full description of the missing girl.

"We have a snapshot of Lucy," said Mrs. Armitage, "if that would be of any help, Inspector."

"Why, of course," exclaimed Sylvia; "she was in that group Mr. Jam Singh took in the garden."

"That couldn't possibly be of any assistance," interposed her father.

"Well, Edward," said his wife, "the Inspector might as well have a look at it. It's in the album among the old *Graphics* and *Punches* in that cupboard."

"I moved all the books out of that

cupboard a week ago," her husband replied.

Hugh in the meantime continued to stroll about aimlessly, taking little notice of the conversation. His eye fell on a small knob projecting from the wall by the fireplace. That knob, he knew, was on the door of the cupboard. The door was flush with the wall and covered with the same patterned paper, so that it was almost concealed by its incorporation with the general scheme of mural decoration. Hugh had noticed such cupboards in Bloomsbury houses before. There was nothing unusual about it. He pulled the knob. The cupboard came open. He looked in. Something had been thrown on to the floor of the cupboard, a sort of large bundle, covered with a linen bedsheet. Hugh took hold of the bedsheet and lifted a portion of it. Some dummy for dressmaking had been thrown into the cupboard. A complete lay figure, a waxen effigy of a girl. How life-like No. How death-like!

Mrs. Armitage was describing Lucy's appearance to the Inspector. Hugh quietly closed the door of the cupboard.

"You needn't trouble to go on with your description, Mrs. Armitage."

"And why not?"

"The Inspector can judge for himself. Lucy hasn't gone far."

"Where is she?"

"In there," he said, pointing to the cupboard.

"My God!" said Mrs. Armitage.

The Inspector moved softly to the cupboard and opened it.

Hugh went quickly to Sylvia's side. "Don't look, Sylvia, dear; I'm afraid we shall find that she's dead."

From the cupboard the Inspector dragged the body of Lucy, and laid it down on the floor. She was wearing a dressing-gown over her night-dress, but there was no suggestion of sleep about that cold, recumbent figure. For a moment there was an awful silence in the room. It was incredible that this rigid, human shape had so recently been alive. Oh, the repellent nothingness, the dreadful isolation, the pathetic loneliness of a dead creature!

Everything still pointed to Lucy.

"She's dead all right," said the Inspector, "I should say she's been dead many hours."

Murmurs of pity and horror fell from the lips of Sylvia and Mrs. Armitage. The Inspector looked curiously at Hugh. There was a faint note of suspicion in his voice, as he asked:

"What made you look in that cupboard?"

"I really don't know. I opened it almost

absent-mindedly . . . I suppose I'd some vague idea of searching for clues."

"Why should you think you might find a clue in there?"

"Oh, I don't know. Just an *impression*," Hugh could not resist this little slap at the officer.

"Nothing more than an impression?"

"Nothing more."

"Well, I can't say I'm so very surprised . . . I thought she might commit suicide, but I imagined she would go to the river."

"You seem very sure that it's suicide."

"Well, obviously it is. An hysterical type like this girl could never stand the strain of murder. She must have committed suicide immediately after the crime. Anyway, we'll get the police surgeon here in a minute, and he'll tell us."

"Yes, but why should the poor girl come down *here* to kill herself?"

The others had all moved towards the cupboard. Mr. Armitage suddenly caught sight of a piece of paper, just outside the cupboard door.

"Look!" he said. "There's a piece of paper here with writing on it." He picked it up and handed it to the Inspector.

The Inspector took the paper and read aloud:

It was him that made me do it. He was a cruel devil. He wouldn't do nothing to help me. I warned him and told him not to drive me too far. I didn't want him to marry me I just wanted help but all he did was to call me wicked names. Perhaps he's sorry now. I am not mad whatever people may say he drove me to it. Heaven have mercy on me Lucy Timson.

There followed a silence. Mr. Armitage broke it.

"A confession," he said simply.

"Well," exclaimed the Inspector, almost cheerfully, "that's that. We don't need the doctors now to tell us whether it was suicide or not, do we? Or who it was did the murder."

"No, it seems clear enough now," said Sylvia. "Oh, dear, *what* a business!"

Mrs. Armitage, like the Inspector, seemed to be quite pleased at the unexpected turn in affairs, though she managed to preserve an outward appearance of solemnity.

"Well," she observed, "the matter shouldn't take long to clear up now. There'll be no reason for policemen and detectives all over the house for weeks on end."

The constable who had taken Jam Singh away reappeared.

"The doctor's here," he announced: "I took him to Reynolds's room."

"Yes, and there's something else here for him to attend to."

Mrs. Armitage was looking at poor Lucy's body with aversion.

"Can't you . . . can't you move this . . . ?" she asked.

"Well, it isn't usual, but it might be more convenient all round."

"There's the back room across the hall we don't use much," suggested Mrs. Armitage.

"Very well. Rogers, give him a hand will you?"

The two constables gently picked up the corpse and carried it from the room.

"Poor Lucy!" sighed Sylvia. "One can't help feeling pity for her!"

"Pity for a murderess? I'm ashamed of you, Sylvia," cried her inexorable mother.

"Yes, even though she was a murderess," replied Sylvia, quietly.

"Sylvia," mused Hugh, "you are quite sure she was?"

"There seems to be no doubt of it now, Hugh."

"It stands to reason, doesn't it?" insisted Mrs. Armitage; "I should have said there was no argument about it, wouldn't you, Ed?"

"No argument at all, m'dear," her husband replied.

"Then you're all agreed," said Hugh, with an implication that he was not so certain.

The Inspector looked up from his note-book.

"Still trying to make a Sherlock Holmes of yourself, Mr. Bromilow, in spite of this confession?"

"D'you think I might be allowed to have a look at that paper?"

The Inspector looked quizzically at Hugh, but nevertheless handed him the paper.

"If it amuses you, but I'm afraid looking at it won't alter its meaning."

Hugh scrutinised the paper. "By Jove, wait a moment!" he cried excitedly. "Looking at it *has* altered it! Look at this first sentence—'It was him that made me do it.' She begins the sentence, the word 'it,' with a small 'i'. See?"

"She was an uneducated girl," argued the Inspector. "That sort very often forget to write capital letters. Besides, you can see that she made a mess at the beginning of the sentence. She wrote a word which she crossed out, and then began 'it was him that made me do it.' That's the obvious reason why she didn't begin with a capital letter."

Hugh was unconvinced, and obviously excited. "But it isn't the real reason. . . . Oh, don't you see . . .?"

"Inspector," said Mrs. Armitage, "do you mind if I go to my room now? I've got a splitting headache. Thank you so much. Sylvia, do you think you could find me some *eau de cologne*?"

"May I?"

"By all means, Miss Armitage."

Sylvia followed her mother out of the room. In the meantime Hugh had jotted down what Lucy had written on a scrap of notepaper. He also examined the original piece of paper very thoroughly before he handed it back to the inspector.

"Well," asked the latter, with biting sarcasm, "may we expect some startling developments?"

"Possibly."

"The brilliant amateur's going to startle the blundering professional, eh?"

"Believe me," Hugh remonstrated, "I entirely appreciate your efficiency and experience. But I've been convinced from the beginning that there's some strange undercurrent in this crime. I can't give you my reasons yet, I confess. But my conviction is absolute."

"Well, it's a free country; you're entitled to your convictions."

Something Hugh could not define had taken hold of him, some power outside of himself seemed to be driving him, goading him on to a certain solution of this mystery, for mystery there assuredly was. Mr. Armitage had stood all the while silently in the room. His attitude was, as usual, that of a man who accepted all the queer tricks that Fate could play with a kind of incurious resignation. One would have imagined he had merely read an account of the murder in the newspaper, rather than that it had happened under his own roof. "These things *do* happen," his expression seemed to say. "It's happened this time to people we know. Very terrible, of course, but . . . these things *do* happen."

Said Hugh to the Inspector: "I'm afraid I must appear interfering and absurdly sceptical, but I can't help that. I never thought that association with a crime would affect me in this way, but you see I suddenly find myself possessed with a strange fever."

"Fever, Mr. Bromilow?" asked Edward Armitage.

"Yes, a fever to get at what I believe is the truth. The truth that I somehow expect to be considerably different from our friend the Inspector's truth. And, at the risk of making a most awful fool of myself,

I'm going to try to justify my annoying attitude and discover that hidden truth."

The Inspector shrugged his shoulders, and smiled. He had no further time to waste; he wanted to see the doctor.

"Well," he said, "all I can say is good luck."

And he went out, leaving Hugh and Mr. Armitage alone.

Hugh continued to pace the room, deep in thought. Mr. Armitage watched him with what appeared to be a kind of fatherly solicitude.

"Do you know, if I were you, I shouldn't bother my head puzzling over this any more, Mr. Bromilow." It was something between a piece of advice and a gentle reproof. Hugh had heard him speak to Sylvia in the same tone. It was as far as her father ever got in the way of admonishment.

"I'm sorry, but I can't chuck it up now, Mr. Armitage. I've got too many pieces in my hand. It only needs two or three other pieces to fit the jig-saw together."

"H'm"—Mr. Armitage was beginning, it seemed, to be mildly interested. "May I make so bold as to ask what pieces you have already?"

"Firstly, this confession. It's a fraud."

Mr. Armitage assumed an incredulous air.

"You mean to say Lucy didn't write it?" he asked.

"Lucy wrote it all right, but she wrote much more. Obviously that letter of hers was written on the front page of a double sheet of notepaper. The words '*it was him that made me do it*' were in the *middle* of a sentence that really began on the front page of the notepaper.''— Hugh was beginning to speak rapidly and excitedly—"The word scratched out wasn't scratched out by Lucy, but by someone else. It was a connecting word with the previous page, and the word was *that*. The sentence ran, 'So and so, and so and so,' that it was him that made me do it.'"

"Aren't you making rather wild guesses?"

"No; I've got the proof. Before the Inspector arrived I had a little reconnoitre on my own in Lucy's room. Amongst other things, I found this in the fireplace."

Hugh produced a small scrap of paper from his waistcoat pocket.

"What is it?" asked Armitage, without much show of curiosity.

"The charred corner of a piece of notepaper exactly corresponding to the half on which Lucy's confession was written. On it, in the same scrawling handwriting, is the one word 'know'—K.N.O.W.—only one word can come after 'know'—'*know that*.'

I think, therefore, the whole sentence was
something like this. 'I want everyone to
know that it was him that made me do it.'"

"Well?" said Armitage. He implied
that he did not see that. Hugh's discovery
materially altered the case.

"My point is, that the confession was
originally written on two pages. It was
merely the last letter of a suicide who
wanted people to know who was responsible,
so that when her body was found that person
responsible would be disgraced."

"I see what you mean." Armitage still
seemed to look on the matter from a de-
tached point-of-view.

"There isn't much point in disgracing a
man you intend to murder, is there?" urged
Hugh.

"She might want to justify the murder."

"Possibly; but why destroy that page of
the confession which would show even more
clearly how justified she was? I tell you
——" Hugh was speaking now with growing conviction and emphasis—"that Lucy
didn't destroy that page. It was destroyed
by someone who wanted to fasten the
murder on to Lucy, and by someone who
saw that if the two pages of the confession
were found, it would point to simple suicide
alone—not murder as well."

"I see . . . so you suggest. . . ."

"I *believe* that someone found Lucy dead, with her confession of suicide—saw the opportunity in the second page to suggest murder and destroyed the first page—and that someone, Mr. Armitage, was the person who committed the murder."

"It strikes me as rather far-fetched, Mr. Bromilow."

"Wait a minute. I can bring it a little closer than that. Now we come to the second piece in the puzzle—Lucy's extraordinary behaviour last night."

"I see no connection."

"She certainly wanted us to see that she was going into Reynolds's room, but that wasn't the chief thing she wanted. What she wanted most was that we should think it was *Lucy* going into Reynolds's room. You see that woman *wasn't* Lucy!"

"You can't possibly know——"

"Why had she got a shawl over her head? Because she wasn't taking the risk of her face being seen, that's why."

Armitage was beginning to show a little more interest, but apparently he would rather have let the matter rest. It had been a most unpleasant affair—most deplorable, but it was all cleared up and done with, fortunately.

"I don't see how you can say it wasn't Lucy just because she wanted you and

Sylvia to see her going into Reynolds's room," he argued. "If she intended to murder him, and then to kill herself, she naturally didn't want anyone else to be wrongly suspected. It's quite likely she wanted to be seen, merely as a corroboration of her written confession."

"But without that confession," Hugh went on, quickly, "I couldn't have come to that conclusion, but having decided that there *is* someone who wants to make everyone think that Lucy did the murder, it follows as a natural sequence. The person who destroyed the missing page of the confession, and the person Sylvia and I saw on the landing wasn't Lucy, but some other woman, and that woman murdered Joseph Reynolds."

"Some other woman?"

"Some other woman who knew this house reasonably well—the positions of Lucy's and Reynolds's rooms—the existence of that cupboard over there, which, after all, isn't very obvious."

Armitage turned Hugh's words over in his mind.

"Quite," he assented; "but it can't be "—his tone turned suddenly to one of dismay and consternation—"you don't think it's someone in the house now?"

"I can't say."

"Impossible! Sylvia, my wife, Miss Snell? Impossible!"

Miss Snell. Fatuous, grotesque, boring, muddle-headed Miss Snell. And in the same house a meek and inoffensive Indian student and a stodgy, beefy, commonplace commercial traveller. The two latter members of some secret organization for smuggling dope into the country. Nothing could be more wildly improbable on the face of it. Then, could Miss Snell, Hugh wondered, his thoughts suddenly diverted into an entirely new channel, be also a member of the organization? And Reynolds had got to be "put out of the way" because he couldn't be trusted? Was *anyone* to be left out of his calculations? Surely it couldn't be Miss Snell. Hugh's thoughts thus wandered into a maëlstrom of wild speculation, from which he was aroused by the unmistakable voice of Miss Snell herself. Both occupants of the room turned and stared at her.

"Oh, you're surprised to see me back again," she simpered; "but I suddenly felt remorse at leaving Mr. Singh in his suffering. When a man, however wicked or depraved, is ill or injured, it's a woman's place to look after him."

"I'm sure that's very thoughtful of you, Miss Snell, but——"

"I've bought some lanoline for his leg,"

the spinster chattered on; "I'm afraid it won't mend the break, that would be almost too much to expect, wouldn't it? But it may slightly relieve the pain. I've always found it invaluable for sunburn, and a cousin of mine in Brazil swears by——"

"A cousin of yours *where?*" asked Hugh, sharply.

Miss Snell was completely taken aback by his tone.

"A cousin of mine in Brazil," she repeated.

"Brazil?" exclaimed Hugh, wildly.

"Yes, Brazil, and why not, Mr. Bromilow?"

"Brazil! Brazil!" Hugh almost shouted; "Now where on earth . . . .?"

Miss Snell backed away from Hugh, timidly. "How very peculiar!" she exclaimed. Really, these authors seemed to be a bit touched. She was rather anxious to get out of his presence.

"Well, as Mr. Singh isn't here——"

"He was taken away by the police, I understand," said Armitage.

"Oh, well, in that case——"

"Brazil!" the word came in a triumphant yell from Hugh. "I've got it!" he shouted. *"Brazil—where the nuts come from!"*

Nuts? What was he raving about? Nuts? Quite certain that Hugh had gone off his own nut, Miss Snell hurried out of the room.

"Don't you see, Mr. Armitage?" shouted Hugh, intensely excited, "that famous line, 'Brazil, where the nuts come from,' in *Charley's Aunt.*"

"No, I don't see."

"Charley's Aunt!" Hugh continued. "Charley's Aunt! *A man dressed up as a woman,* now don't you see? I never thought of that, I only thought of some other woman, but a man dressed up . . . it's been done before."

"What's been done before?" asked Armitage, a trifle impatiently.

"Masquerading as a woman to avoid suspicion of a murder . . . it's in a book of crimes by H. B. Irving . . . I've got it upstairs . . . 'A Book of Remarkable Criminals.' It's an amazing story, but absolutely true. About a little French tailor who murdered a woman for her money, and then impersonated her himself, so that her disappearance shouldn't be noticed. Wait a moment——" Hugh moved towards the door and opened it —"the book's in my room, I'll go and fetch it, you shall see for yourself. No—" he came back into the room, closing the door—"no, now I come to think of it, it isn't in my room. I brought it down here yesterday morning with some papers in it. I left it down here. Yes, I remember now, because after lunch, when I came in, someone had picked it up and was reading it, and I didn't like to disturb them . . . now . . . who was reading that book?"

"Perhaps they've returned it to your room."

"No, I'm sure they haven't; if it's anywhere it would be lying about here. . . ."

Hugh was searching around among the papers on the table. Armitage's attaché case was lying on the table where he had left it when he first entered the room. Unthinkingly, Hugh put his hand on the case to move it.

"Leave that case alone, damn you!" shouted Armitage, in a sharp, startled, unfamiliar tone. Hugh stared at the man in bewilderment. Armitage's face was ugly and threatening, and pale. What was the little chap so wild about? As if he'd intended to open the case! Why. . . .

The case lay on the table. Armitage's hand went to it—then Hugh's. Hugh retained his grip on the case and the two men faced each other across it. Hugh's astonishment at the other's behaviour had turned to a realization of the reason for it.

Hugh looked into Armitage's eyes.

"It was you!" he said in level, forceful

tones; "it was you who was reading that book yesterday afternoon. I remember now . . . that book is here in this case. My God, I can see it now, I can see it in your eyes. *It was you who killed Joseph Reynolds!*"

Mr. Armitage straightened himself up. With an effort he regained his self-control. He took a packet of cigarettes out of his pocket. He had suddenly completely regained his self-possession.

"You must be raving mad, Mr. Bromilow," he said, with absolute calm.

"You know I'm not. Nothing you say could possibly hide the truth now. And . . . *look!*"

Armitage was inserting a cigarette in a wooden holder.

Hugh suddenly sprang forward and snatched the cigarette from his hand.

"Look!" he cried, almost breathless with excitement. "The Blue Line cigarettes, an unusual brand. The cigarette ends that I found in Lucy's room! Those unaccountable cigarette ends that had been fitted into a cigarette holder—*your* cigarette holder!"

"The merest coincidence!" Armitage exclaimed.

"Will you say then, that the fact that my book, this 'Book of Remarkable

Criminals' is here in your case now, is also
a coincidence?"

"I tell you the book is not in the case!"
Armitage declared fiercely.

"Open it then and show me!" Hugh
challenged him.

"I'll do nothing of the sort. I refuse to
humour such hysterical nonsense."

"Then I shall!"

In the same instant both men made a
sudden grab at the case. Fiercely, for a
moment or two, they fought for its possession. Then the case flew open and a book
fell out of it to the floor. Quick as thought
Hugh snatched the volume up.

"'A Book of Remarkable Criminals,' by
H. B. Irving!" he said, triumphantly. He
opened the book. "And here, at the case
of the little tailor which I quoted, is the
page turned down."

White as death, Armitage staggered to a
chair and sat down. Hugh continued, in a
white heat of concentration, reconstructing
the crime as he spoke.

"Somehow or other you never went to
Brighton. You came back here secretly.
You found Lucy dead . . . you read her
confession . . . you saw your opportunity
. . . you impersonated Lucy and you murdered Joseph Reynolds."

Mr. Armitage was staring straight ahead

of him with a fixed, dazed, expressionless gaze. Completely carried away, Hugh went on with ruthless, deliberate insistence: "It's the truth, isn't it? You've got to tell me. You'll never have another minute's peace unless you tell me. You may get away with this all right, but you'll have to tell someone some day. You won't be able to help yourself, you aren't strong enough. Come on, tell me now. You murdered Joseph Reynolds."

Edward Armitage looked into Hugh's eyes, hypnotized, hopeless, defeated.

"Yes!"

There was a long pause. A church bell began to ring, and then another.

Hugh spoke quietly. He was emotionally, almost physically exhausted.

"Why? In God's name, why?"

Yes! Bromilow was right. He would have had to speak. It was almost a relief to be found out so soon, to be able to tell everything.

"Because of my wife," Armitage replied, brokenly; "I found out about her and Reynolds."

"Your wife and Reynolds? Yes—yes—of course; her behaviour when she discovered him dead, and then her fear of the questions. In a way I half suspected."

Armitage went on quietly. "I loved my

wife. No one will ever know how much I loved her. I didn't know myself until I discovered yesterday that another man had stolen her from me."

"You didn't discover until yesterday?"

"I came in here and found him kissing her. I knew in an instant, from the way he kissed her, that he possessed her—that she was completely in his power—and had been for a long time."

"They didn't see you?"

"I don't know. I was just sort of numbed and cold. I talked quite mechanically and then I went out to go to Victoria. It wasn't until I slammed the front door that—the thing happened to me."

"What thing?"

"That numbed, cold feeling began to thaw. Gradually at first, then with an awful rush that made me feel sick. I walked along Malim Street to the corner where the buses stop, and when I got there my legs shook so, I had to hang on to the railings. They say"—his face was distorted with anguish—"they say that jealousy is green, don't they? It isn't, it's red, flaming red! My legs grew steady again, I began to walk. I walked and walked—thinking all the time. Thoughts that only made things worse . . . about my wife . . . and those early days when I first knew her. And about the days before I knew her . . . when Reynolds. . . ." He paused, overcome with emotion, and then went on brokenly: "Gradually a vague plan came into my head. First of all I went into a shop and telephoned Fred Spencer."

"Ah, yes; your friend at Brighton, your alibi."

"Spencer is a life-long friend. I knew that I could depend on him, even in a case of murder. I—I came back here while they were all at dinner. No one saw me. I went right up to the top of the house, to the box-room opposite Lucy's room, and stayed there in the dark, with the door half open. After about an hour, I heard Lucy come up. After a bit I looked out of the box-room and saw Lucy's door half open. There was a light in the room, but not a sound coming from it. I thought perhaps she'd gone down-stairs without my hearing her and left the light on. I looked through the crack of the door. Lucy was half hanging, half lying off the edge of the bed. I went in—you know pretty well what I found there."

"She was dead *then*, I suppose?"

"Yes; I sat thinking, and then I found myself remembering that story in that book of yours, which I had been reading after lunch. I had slipped it into my case to read on the journey, and the more I thought of that story, the more I saw what an opportunity I had. I dressed up in her things and I waited. When you two came in, *I made sure that you'd both see me on the landing*. It worked perfectly—like clockwork."

As Armitage told the story his calmness returned. He finished on a note of satisfaction. Here, of course, was a man demented.

Hugh was astounded. The psychology of Edward Armitage so resembled that of many of the notorious murderers whose histories and characters he had studied for years.

"What I don't understand is," said Hugh, "why, after you had killed Reynolds, did you bring the dead body of Lucy downstairs, instead of leaving her in her own room?"

"Well, you see, I found Lucy dead at a quarter to nine . . . the murder wasn't committed until midnight at the earliest . . . a lapse of over three hours. It occurred to me that the doctors, when they found Lucy, might be able to tell that she died long before midnight, and so upset my schemes for fastening the murder on her. So I got panicky and decided that if possible, Lucy should never be found."

"But you must have known she would have been found sooner or later if you had left her in that cupboard?"

"Of course; but I wasn't going to leave

her there. In the meantime, if she were found in the cupboard, that confession would serve as sufficient shield for me."

"I see," said Hugh.

Hugh was amazed, and in some queer way fascinated by this uncanny experience. Face to face with a murderer, calmly confessing his crime, recounting the details of it, and it was he himself who had forced the whole story from the guilty man's lips. Armitage was in a dream, living again his awful experiences. Neither of them noticed that Mrs. Armitage and Sylvia had entered the room. The latter was about to address her father, but he went on speaking and his words struck both Sylvia and her mother dumb with horror.

"It took me hours, so it seemed," they heard him say, "carrying Lucy's body down all those stairs . . . that awful dead night . . . and trying not to make a sound. I was terribly exhausted. I'd used every ounce of strength in my body when I stabbed Reynolds . . . I was on the verge of collapse . . . I don't know what I'm to do . . . I was driven to it . . . God help me! . . . driven to it . . . !"

Mrs. Armitage rushed towards her husband, with a dreadful cry.

"Edward! Edward! What are you saying? Am I going mad?"

"Daddy!" cried Sylvia. . . . "Don't! Don't! It isn't true! It can't be!"

Hugh was on his feet, terribly distressed that the ghastly truth about Armitage should be revealed to his wife—and to Sylvia. Sylvia knew . . . it was unbearable!

Armitage faced his wife and daughter, dazed with the tragedy of it all. "It's true . . ." he said, in a strange, choked voice, "quite true . . . I did it. I killed him . . . Lucy had killed herself . . . I knew that . . . and I tried to put it all on to her. But he's found out . . . it's all over now!"

Mrs. Armitage and Sylvia uttered incoherent cries of distress, incredulous, protesting. They could not believe their own ears.

"Hush, for heaven's sake!" exclaimed Hugh, "no one need ever know but us . . . they all think Lucy did it. . . . For God's sake, keep calm, no one need ever know!"

He had the greatest difficulty in calming them. In fact, a minute or so later when the Inspector came back unexpectedly, Mrs. Armitage was still sobbing loudly in her daughter's arms. Sylvia, too, was weeping.

"You must excuse these ladies, Inspector, it's been a bit too much for their nerves as you see," said Hugh calmly.

"I think you must admit they've been pretty plucky."

"Very plucky indeed!" agreed the Inspector. "And now the matter's all cleared up, it's only natural they should relieve their feelings. I don't intrude, I hope."

"Not at all, Inspector," Hugh rejoined; "and Mr. Armitage, too—you can see he's feeling the strain."

"I can quite understand that. But you're a pretty cool sort of customer, aren't you, Mr. Bromilow?"

"Well, you see," Hugh explained with a smile; "it hasn't happened in my house."

"Ah!" was the Inspector's comprehensible comment. "Well, if I'm not *dee tro*, as the French say, I've just looked in to tell you that the doctor's made his examination and he says there's no question about it. It's suicide all right, as I thought. Poison, the doctor says. Just as well she killed herself, she saved herself a murder trial and the swinging afterwards. So don't upset yourself, Mrs. Armitage, you won't be bothered much more. We shall want you to hold yourselves ready, all of you I expect, to give formal evidence at the inquest, but that's all. And the newspapers won't trouble you over much. After all, there's no mystery for them to work up a stunt over, is there? Unless, of course, our friend Sherlock Holmes here has any fresh light to throw upon the case? May I ask, Mr. Bromilow, if you have discovered this amazing . . . what was it . . . er . . . hidden truth?"

There was a few moments complete silence. Hugh managed to assume a sheepish, downcast air, as he replied:

"No; I've discovered nothing."

"You're sure?"

"Quite sure."

"And your . . . *impressions?* "

"Well—merely what you said, Inspector. Just impressions, that's all."

"Then you admit——"

"I admit that you're right, and I'm entirely wrong."

"Now, that's very sporting of you, Mr. Bromilow. Well, good-morning all. You won't forget, please, to hold yourselves in readiness to give evidence. . . . Good-day . . . good-day!"

The Inspector left those four people alone. The father, a self-confessed murderer, goaded into the crime by the infidelity of his wife. She, with the full knowledge that her own guilt had driven her husband— her loyal, patient, devoted husband to this terrible deed. And their daughter , . . who had now got to suffer for life for their irretrievable sins. And the man who loved their daughter . . . what did it matter to him? . . . he loved her. That was all.

Mrs. Armitage was the first to speak. She spoke in a dull, despairing tone.

"What are we going to do?"

"Nothing," said Hugh. "Nothing."

"But you know now?"

"All four of us know." Hugh spoke quietly, and with a courage that gave hope and courage to the others. "Murder is a terrible thing. But now that all the facts have come to light, we know that . . ."

He was going to say that Reynolds deserved death if anyone did, but a certain amount of pity he could not help feeling for Mrs. Armitage restrained him.

"It was my fault, Mr. Bromilow," said Mrs. Armitage. "Yes, my fault, Mr. Bromilow. Edward did it because. . . ."

"Your husband did it," continued Hugh, "because he loved you, Mrs. Armitage. His love for you drove him to do a desperate, horrible thing. Think, Mrs. Armitage, other men have loved you . . . in a way . . . but, I tell you both, that if you really want it to, this awful secret can turn itself into something far from awful . . . you understand?"

Mrs. Armitage walked towards the door unsteadily.

"Yes, I think I understand . . . Edward . . . !"

"Oh, my dear!" murmured Armitage, in a low, heartbroken tone.

He went to her side. Then she turned and looked at Hugh.

"But, Mr. Bromilow . . . why should you be involved?"

Hugh looked at Sylvia. "I've the strongest reason in the world, Mrs. Armitage," he answered.

"I see!" said Mrs. Armstrong quietly. And she took her husband's hand in hers and led him from the room.

"Oh, Sylvia!" Hugh exclaimed. "Can you ever forgive me?"

"Forgive you?"

"If it hadn't been for my infernal curiosity we should none of us have ever known."

"I think it's better we do know. Better for us all."

"It's not better for me, Sylvia. There was something I wanted to ask you, and now I can't ask you because I shall feel that this secret between us is putting you at a disadvantage. I can't ask you now."

"You don't have to."

"What do you mean?"

"You silly! Didn't you know that it's the women who always do the asking?

The poor men think it's them; but it's the woman really."

"Sylvia, darling," he murmured tenderly. He took her in his arms and kissed her. A ray of sunshine suddenly flooded the room with radiance.

"Hugh, look! The sun is shining! Let's go out. The house is horrid after this dreadful morning. Let's go out into the park."

"Yes," he assented. "Let's go out into the sunshine."

* * * * * *

And now let us remember that when we first met Sylvia Armitage she was cheerfully helping with the washing-up. A dull job, washing-up, for very dull people. The only person in the house who wasn't dull was Hubert Bromilow, that good-looking young author who *would* be superior and write all those high-brow plays that nobody wanted to buy! And life, on the whole, was quite satisfactory, but rather on the dull and monotonous side. Until the others had all gone upstairs after lunch to play cards and she had been left alone in the dining-room with Hugh. Then life had begun to be a bit more thrilling.

"Look here, Sylvia," he had said, suddenly, "I've got something to tell you. Something I *must* tell you."

"Yes?"

"I've been wanting to tell you for a long time. But . . . well, it's a secret. Still, it's a secret I'd like you to share because . . . because you don't understand. . . . I'm not altogether the sort of 'Johnny-Head in-Air' sort of fellow you seem to think me. That's only one side to my character."

"Don't wander from the point. What is it you want to tell me?"

"You'll be terribly thrilled . . . at least I hope you will."

"I'm thrilled already."

"Are you? That's splendid. Sylvia, if you only knew how I've been longing to tell you that I. . . ."

"What?"

"I . . . no . . . I shan't tell you yet. Not until you've admitted that I *can* write a jolly good thrilling sort of play that would appeal to . . . to the vast crowd of ordinary, everyday people. A play that would make pots of money for me and . . . and . . . well, you said just now, 'Why not write a play about the people in this house?' Well, it's a wet afternoon; I'll do it now, between lunch and tea!"

"Bravo!" cried Sylvia. "*Now*. This minute!"

"Yes—*now*, this minute. Can you use your imagination?"

"I don't know. I hope so."

"Act One . . . the scene is—wait a moment—the scene is *this room*. Yes, *this room*. Why not? Are you ready?"

"Yes, I'm ready!" cried Sylvia, carried away by his enthusiasm. "Go on."

"Very well, then. The curtain rises. The scene is this room. It is late in the afternoon. Outside the rain is descending in torrents. The door opens very slowly, and Jam Singh creeps very stealthily into the room. . . ."

PART FIVE

PART FIVE

"LET's go out into the sunshine."

* * * * * *

"And that's the end of the play?" asked Sylvia.

"Yes," said Hugh.

"We two going out into the park?"

"Yes."

"I liked it awfully."

"Did you really?" he asked eagerly.

"And to make it all up on the spur of the moment like that!" She gazed at him in wide-eyed admiration.

"I only did it to please you."

"I know. It was sweet of you."

"But. . . ." pleaded Hugh. "Did you really like it all? Even that bit about us in the moonlight?"

"I liked that best of all," she answered, frankly.

"Oh, Sylvia——" and this time he really actually *did* take her in his arms. "Then you do really . . . you mean that you . . ."

"Of course I do, silly!"

And this time he really, actually kissed her.

"And you don't think I'm superior any more?"

"My darling, no! How could anyone think you superior after making up a plot like that?"

"Yes . . . quite," he assented, with a sardonic smile.

"What's the play called?" she asked.

"Does that matter?"

"Certainly, it's half the battle. Call it something exciting—it doesn't matter what, so long as it makes your flesh creep when you look at the programme."

"Well, how about *The House of*——, no, that's been used before. Let's think of other boarding house plays. *At Mrs. Beam's. At Mrs. Armitage's*—how's that?"

"No; I think that's rather dull."

"Then there was *The Passing of the Third Floor Back*—I say, how about *The Second Floor Crime*—no, that's no good. I know! *Murder on the Second Floor!* How's that?"

"Oh, yes, that's *lovely!*"

"Thank God for that!" exclaimed Hugh with relief.

"It's a topping play, Hugh. **I** love it!"

"So do I, Sylvia. *I* love the play, darling because it's given you to me. My sweet, we'll be married terribly, terribly soon, won't we?"

"*Look out!*" exclaimed Sylvia, somewhat irrelevantly. As a matter of fact she had heard someone coming downstairs. In another moment Mr. Reynolds, the man who had been murdered on the second floor without ever suspecting it, came into the room "as large as life." Sylvia involuntarily uttered a scream. "Oh, how you startled me!" she panted.

"Sorry, I'm sure!" Reynolds apologized. "Did I come in very quietly?"

"No," Sylvia replied, staring at him with what he thought was a most unaccountable look of profound commiseration. "I was thinking of your poor throat. I'm so glad it's better."

"Throat?" exclaimed Reynolds, rather testily. "I don't understand. There's nothing the matter with my throat."

Sylvia was suddenly overcome with confusion. Hugh watched her with amusement. She was being very complimentary not only to him as an author, but also as an actor if she had been carried away to this extent.

"No!" she said. "Of course not, Mr. Reynolds. I thought you said you had a sore throat after lunch!"

"I said my *corns* were giving me jip. I didn't mention my throat. But I don't mind telling you what I want is a nice cup of tea. I've got a bit of a headache after Miss Snell's overcalling."

By this time Mrs. Armitage had drifted into the room. "Who's got a headache?" she said. Sylvia ran to her mother and kissed her with sudden, impulsive tenderness.

"Mummy, darling," she cried, "oh, Mummy, don't worry dear, it's all right."

"All right . . . my dear Sylvia!"

"Oh . . . I mean . . . it's only Mr. Reynolds has a slight headache and wants his tea . . . oh, Mummy!"

Mrs. Armitage looked bewildered. "What *is* the matter, Sylvia," she asked.

Sylvia again had to recover herself. "Nothing, Mummy, nothing—only it's nice to see you again," she said rather lamely.

"Well, I never, you funny girlie! Did you say you had a headache, Mr. Reynolds? I'll go and get you an aspirin."

"No, no, Mrs. Armitage," Reynolds protested. "Not on any account, thank you. It'll pass off of its own accord. I won't have anything to do with aspirin—no, nor any other form of dope."

"Oh, I'm so glad to hear that!" Sylvia exclaimed, joyfully.

Then Miss Snell joined the group. "Well, I'm ready for my tea, I must say!" she announced; "such an enjoyable game, Mr. Bromilow. I'm afraid I overcalled once or twice rather badly. However, I managed to escape by the skin of my teeth."

"Of your *teeth!*" said Sylvia, choking with laughter.

"Yes; a comical expression, is it not? It always makes me laugh. But it's slang, I'm afraid! Ah, not gone yet, Mr. Armitage? I suppose you'll have tea before you start, then?"

Mr. Armitage, who had strolled in for a cup of tea, crossed the room to the concealed cupboard by the fireplace. Sylvia watched him, fascinated with horror.

Mr. Armitage opened the cupboard door. "Oh, there it is!" he exclaimed.

"*What is?*" Sylvia asked, shuddering.

"My old raincoat. I was thinking of taking it with me to Brighton to-night."

"Daddy," said Sylvia nervously, "you'll make certain of catching the train, won't you?"

"Why, of course, my dear!" and Mr. Armitage sat down in an armchair and began to read an evening paper he had brought in with him.

"Oh, am I too late for tea!" It was the voice of Jam Singh.

"No, we haven't had it yet, Mr. Singh."

"Oh, I'm glad of that. I am ready for mine. Oh, by the way, Mrs. Armitage, would you be so kind as to replace the soapdish in my room—someone has broken it."

"That girl again!" exclaimed Mrs. Armitage.

"Well, of course, I do not suppose anyone else has been in the room," said Jam Singh, "and I do not wish to get anyone into trouble. But everything points to Lucy."

"Well, the last time you said that, Mr Singh——" Sylvia began, evincing a most unaccountable excitement.

"I do not remember saying it before," said Singh. "Was it when my tooth-brush——?"

"Yes, the tooth-brush," Sylvia assented suddenly. "Still, the least said soonest mended. We don't want to fix the blame on Lucy."

"It is not of much account, anyway. Oh, Miss Snell, here is your library book."

"Oh, thank you so much! What have they given me this time?"

"'The Triangular Circle,' Leonard Swanage's latest book."

"Well, there's a funny coincidence!" exclaimed Mr. Armitage, looking up from his paper; "here's a notice of Leonard Swanage's latest play, produced last night."

"Read it, Edward," said Mrs. Armitage, whose interest in theatrical matters still occasionally flickered up again.

Mr. Armitage proceeded to read: "'Scenes of the greatest enthusiasm marked the final curtain of Leonard Swanage's latest thriller produced at the Duke's Theatre last night. As usual, Mr. Swanage has set out to thrill and, as usual, he has succeeded. Even his title provokes a shiver, for what more harrowing title than *Murder on the Second Floor* could——'"

"*What?*" Sylvia almost shouted.

"*Murder on the Second Floor*," continued Mr. Armitage. "'What more harrowing title than *Murder on the Second Floor* could be conceived? The scene is laid in a Bloomsbury boarding-house.'"

"Well, I never!" exclaimed Mrs. Armitage.

"Well, I'm glad it's not *our* house, my dear!" laughed Mr. Armitage. "Just listen: 'A murder, a suicide, the discovery of a parlourmaid's dead body in a cupboard, are among a few of the most hair-raising incidents.'"

"Any pretty girls in it?" asked Reynolds.

"It doesn't say—wait a minute—oh, that's only about the acting. 'At the same time—' he read on—'we can't help feeling that such a fine craftsman as Leonard Swanage should waste his talents in writing plays whose chief appeal is to the lower and more debased side of the public's taste.'"

"Well, really, I call that most unnecessary!" exclaimed Miss Snell, indignantly; "I always enjoy his plays and I'm sure my taste isn't low or debased."

A timid knock sounded on the door.

"Come in!" said Mrs. Armitage.

Lucy Timson came into the room.

"What a relief!" murmured Sylvia to Hugh.

"Oh, lor, mum!" Lucy cried, "I've been and gone and taken the tea up to the drawing-room. I thought, with your card-playing, you'd——"

"You know we only have tea in the drawing-room on Sundays."

"Shall I bring it down here, mum?"

"Let's go up, Mrs. A., it'll save time," suggested Reynolds; "I'm dying for a cup of tea."

This suggestion was adopted. All the occupants of the room, except Hugh and Sylvia, adjourned for tea to the drawing-room. As soon as they had gone, Sylvia picked up the newspaper which her father had left behind, and read the criticism again with feverish interest. She looked at Hugh with half-incredulous, wide, admiring eyes.

"So *you* are Leonard Swanage, after all!"

"I'm afraid so. I'm terribly sorry."

"But I don't understand."

"I wanted 'copy' for this play that was

produced last night. I came here and found that besides 'copy' I was able to obtain the most glorious escape from secretaries, editors, actors, actresses, theatrical managers and literary agents. I finished *Murder on the Second Floor* long ago, but I couldn't leave here. You know the reason why I stayed on, extraordinarily happy. I got out some of my earlier idealistic work and began tinkering at it again."

"But why pretend that you made up the play on the spur of the moment?"

"I wanted to impress you, and I thought it would impress you more than if I simply said to you: 'Oh, but I am Leonard Swanage.' That would have been rather tame, wouldn't it?"

"Yes, I suppose it would."

"I've been a deceitful swine—it was your fault, darling, you made me unscrupulous. All's fair in love and thingamybob, you know. Forgive me, my sweet."

Sylvia could not resist affecting a few moments' hesitation. Then she murmured:

"I suppose I shall have to."

"Isn't it marvellous to think," he asked, his arms around her, "that you're going to be the great Mrs. Leonard Swanage?"

"It's wonderful!" sighed Sylvia; "but, darling," she added thoughtfully, "you know that bit in the paper?"

"Which bit?"

Sylvia picked the newspaper up. "This bit: 'It is a pity that such a fine craftsman should waste his talents on writing plays whose chief appeal is to the lower and more debased side of the public's taste."

"Yes?" he asked, in some surprise. "Well, what about it?"

"Well, will you promise me something, darling?" she pleaded.

"Anything, my love; anything in the world."

"Well, will you promise me, sweetheart, that one day——"

"One day; what?"

"That one day you'll write a really *good* play . . . ?"

Produced in conjunction with
The Readers Library Publishing Co. Ltd.